A Candle at Dusk

E. M. ALMEDINGEN

A Candle at Dusk

Illustrated by

DOREEN ROBERTS

London
OXFORD UNIVERSITY PRESS
1969

Oxford University Press, Ely House, London W. 1

GLASGOW NEW YORK TORONTO MELBOURNE WELLINGTON
CAPE TOWN SALISBURY IBADAN NAIROBI LUSAKA ADDIS ABABA
BOMBAY CALCUTTA MADRAS KARACHI LAHORE DACCA
KUALA LUMPUR SINGAPORE HONG KONG TOKYO

Printed in Great Britain by
Western Printing Services Ltd, Bristol

Author's Note

Abbot Ursin and Defensor are the only historical persons in the story. The Abbey of LiguGé is supposed to have been destroyed by the Arabs in the autumn of 732 when the great battle of Poitiers took place. The abbey's name vanishes from all records for nearly four centuries. When it re-appears, it is no longer an abbey but a priory dependent on a great monastery in the neighbourhood.

The importance of the Frankish victory in 732 came to be minimized in later centuries, but to the contemporaries it was truly a magnificent spring which followed a particularly grim winter.

Defensor's little book, by whichever means it came to be salvaged out of the ruins of the abbey, ended by being something of a best-seller through the Middle Ages. Today, more than three hundred manuscripts of it are preserved in libraries throughout Europe.

Idrun's background is drawn from contemporary sources and so is the neighbouring landscape. The town of Poitiers was indeed ravaged by the Arabs.

In Idrun's childhood and youth very, very few laymen knew their letters. Book-learning was left to clergy and monks. It was Charles Martel's grandson, Charlemagne, who was the first to encourage learning among the laity.

April 1968   E. M. Almedingen

Contents

I

The Broken Crock

Gay April sunlight danced and rippled over the carefully sown rows of beans, turnips, and lettuce. The humming of bees came from the old limes which girdled the broad end of the kitchen-garden. The morning was still young, and the fragile lace of gossamer hung here and there along the thick blackthorn hedge which skirted the little orchard to the left. All over the place lay the strong young fragrance of swelling bud and awakened soil. It was good to be in the open after the stale smokiness of the house, and the two boys, digging in a corner, worked with a will. The younger, aged about ten, wore a dark red tunic and white linen breeches, and his legs were bare. The spade briefly idle, he threw back his flaxen head and stared at the hawthorn hedge with a look of someone cherishing a great secret. The look was true since with the coming of spring, so Idrun thought, his secret gained in strength and colour.

'Ah—it will happen because happen it must,' he thought.

The elder boy wore a drab brown smock which barely covered his bony shoulders and reached just below the knees. Master's son and servant's son, the two were friends, and laughed and sang at their work.

Suddenly the younger lad tossed aside his spade and cried:

'Oh, Gunto, look, look . . .'

On the moist black soil lay a gorgeously painted butterfly, all its colours singing to the sky.

'The first of the year! That means—'

Gunto nodded his ravelled black hair.

'Yes, a wish come true, Idrun. But it looks dead to me.'

'No, no, no—'

Idrun, digging forgotten, knelt and cupped his thin brown hands. The butterfly did not stir. Still kneeling, he held it and at last saw the tremor of a wing.

'I must show it to my mother, Gunto.'

Idrun raced through the kitchen-garden, past the row of out-buildings, to the great yard fronting the old house. A few apple-trees, their tight coral buds gleaming in the sun, stood here and there, but Idrun did not look at them. He halted, aware of a movement between his palms. He spread them open: the lovely wings were rising and falling. Within an instant, the crimson, blue and golden glory vanished in the foliage of the nearest apple-tree.

Idrun stood, biting his lips, since no free-born Frank, so his father had taught him, should ever cry. The butterfly had found a home, but he could never now show it to his mother, and the small disappointment bit into him sharply until it merged into anger. He turned his back on the apple-tree and ambled towards the herb bed against a wall. Nearing it, he stumbled on something and, anger still gripping him, Idrun kicked the thing he could not see and kicked it so hard that it went hurtling against the wall. He halted to see the shards of his mother's favourite herb crock scattered on the young grass.

The golden day shrouded, Idrun knelt and started picking up the pieces to show them to his mother. One of the shards had a jagged edge to it and gashed his left thumb. He stooped low to suck the wound when a familiar voice rang behind him.

Crimson with anger and shame, Idrun leapt to his feet, turned, and saw his mother in her spring gown of grey-blue clasped by a silver buckle at the left shoulder, her fair hair barely visible under a snow-white veil. Idrun stared down at her shapely feet shod in green. He mumbled:

'I'm sorry about the crock—'

'Your thumb,' said Aldis, without looking at the shards. 'Come and I'll bind it up for you.'

Head bent, Idrun followed her to the house. The great ground-floor room, meagrely furnished with oaken trestles, a few benches and a narrow long table, was empty except for two servants

bustling about a cauldron hung over a fire in the middle of the room. The place smelt of wet stone, crushed herbs and a savoury stew. Were it not for the great doors flung wide open, the hall would have been dark; so few and narrow were the slits of the windows.

Aldis mounted a crazy wooden stairway at the end of the hall. In the bedroom, she cleaned the wound, dabbed a spot of dark yellow ointment on it, and then wrapped it up in a piece of linen.

'Thank you, Mother,' Idrun muttered and made for the stairs when Aldis said:

'Be more careful, son. Crocks and pots are not easy to come by these days.'

'Oh—why?'

Aldis sighed.

'Ah so many things—' she murmured, looking away from her son.

Few were the fairs held in Frankland in the early eighth century, and it was not always possible to find what you wanted at the market in Poitiers, a good day's ride from their home. Aldis, herself taciturn, had listened to her husband, the servants, the visitors to the steading. They would talk of poverty, lawlessness, heavy taxes, bad harvests, roads falling into disrepair, money losing its value. Old Sir Martin, their priest, who lived at the mouth of the valley, mumbled on and on about the wrath of God. Out of it all Aldis had gathered that most, if not all, of the country's troubles were due to the Arabs. When still a little girl, she would hear frightening stories about those men who, having gone from wherever they used to live, had stampeded into Spain. True that the rocky heights of the Pyrenees stood between them and Frankland. None the less, it was the Saracens who were responsible for every mishap in the country, including the sudden blindness of Sevra, Aldis's best needlewoman.

The Saracens, Aldis knew, did not believe in Christ, and they were keen on spreading their heathen doctrines all over Southern Europe. She thought their god was called Mohammed, but she was not quite sure.

But she would not tell her son anything. A lad of ten, what would he understand? She repeated in a dull voice, 'Ah so many things,' and then put her hand on Idrun's shoulder.

'Son—'

He stared at her.

'I know what is the matter with you, and so does your father.'

'But—but—I have never told you,' he stammered.

'Never mind how we came to know of it. Ever since you first went to Liguge Abbey, you have wanted it—'

Idrun did not speak, but his cheeks were crimson and his chin shook.

'To be taught letters,' went on Aldis calmly. 'No, son. One day you'll have to look after this place. They would turn you into a monk once they have taught you how to read and write. You understand?'

Idrun stood silent. The day, which had broken in pure gold, was now heavily leaden. He had always known that it would be difficult to get his parents' consent, difficult but, as he had hoped, not impossible. He knew that he could do nothing now, and he had no words to explain the hunger which burned in him to learn as much as his friend at Ligugé, Dom Defensor, the librarian, could teach him. To hold a book and be able to read. . . . To seize a sheet of parchment and a style and to write. . . . What could compare with such happiness? And there was no need for him to become a monk. Did his mother not know that the Count's messengers and tax-collectors were laymen and yet they knew their letters? And who could have given him away? Certainly, not Gunto, and nobody else at Clear Water knew of it.

The place? Yes, Idrun loved it, but he could not see why his being literate should interfere with the work in the fields and elsewhere. His cheeks wild red, he made for the stairway, crossed the great hall, and came out into the sunlight which now said nothing to him.

Aldis watched him go.

'Ah—surely, he'll forget all about it,' she thought comfortably, came down, and called on two serving-women to help her with the cheeses which she meant to take to the ladies of St Cross Abbey at Poitiers.

Clear Water, Aqua Clara, as it used to be known in ancient days, took its name from a small lake slightly to the south-east of the steading. Certainly, the name answered. The stone wall, surrounding the house and the gardens, had nothing forbidding in it, its grey having turned to pale pink and gold. The house had once been a Roman fort, but the Romans had gone long, long ago, and the roseate-grey walls had lost their virginal severity. Idrun's great-grandfather had bought it and much land from the Count of Poitou, and little by little the keep became a house, its very narrow windows, overlooking the great yard, the sole reminders of a stern past. The yard itself looked gay enough in spring and summer, apple and cherry trees planted here and there. To the left of the massive gates ran a whimsical row of out-buildings curving towards the back to the immense kitchen-garden and the orchard. The fields on the slopes of the Smarves Mountains were sown with beans, oats, and barley, but wheat, then very precious in Frank-land, grew within the enclosure. A pond shimmered at the very end of the orchard, its clear waters a merry meeting-place for geese and waterfowl.

To the right of the great gate ran a rough track northwards, the shrub-covered slopes of the Smarves on one side and a larch wood streaked by countless streams on the other. The track wound up and up, and ended by widening into a valley which ran down to the steep banks of the Clain. That track was rather hard of access from the south, and pillage and war, those unending disasters of the early eighth century, passed it by. Clear Water's nearest neigh-bour lived at the very mouth of the valley, old Sir Martin, whose tiny hut stood cheek-by-jowl with the chapel. The parishioners were few: Turgot, the closest friend of Idrun's father, whose farm, Troissant, ran right down to the river bank, and some ten labourers and their wives; a blacksmith, Grifo, whose forge stood idle all too often, and the people of Clear Water.

Sir Martin kept a cow and two pigs, sowed beans and a little corn on a plot behind the chapel, the land being his by courtesy rather than law. Bent-shouldered, untidy, and so small was he that a chasuble given him by the monks reached down to the beaten clay floor of the chapel and he often tripped over it. Yet his smile was endearing and his manner gentle. He would mumble through the Mass, unvest at the foot of the tiny altar, and then shuffle to the door to shed tears of gratitude at the gifts brought by his people. Yet the last time Idrun and his parents went to Mass, Sir Martin wept in sorrow, the tax-collector having taken away one of his pigs to pay for the arrears the old man owed. Berno, Idrun's father, at once promised a pig, and a bag of seeds; but Idrun thought that no tax-collector would ever dare behave so arrogantly at Clear Water because his tall, broad-shouldered father was a man of property, and Aldis came of respectable Gallo–Roman descent and had two great-uncles as bishops in the South and brought a sizable dowry to Berno: linen, two fur coverlets, three cauldrons, a silver chain and two silver spoons of cunning Greek workmanship, and a relic in a finely carved horn box given her by a cousin, a nun at St Cross Abbey at Poitiers. The relic was a tiny piece of St Martin's sandal, and Berno did not think much of it but he never said so.

Southwards from the gate of Clear Water the track ran wide, its edges enamelled gold and blue and pink through the spring and summer months. Some way down, in between straggling thorns and elders, you could see an oval sheet of water, known as Silver Lake. On the other side lay a thick oak coppice. The track, ever widening, ended at the fringe of a great forest with a single rough ride across it. Mal Forest they called it because of robbers and wild beasts prowling up and down its fastnesses. Beyond it could be glimpsed the towers and roofs of Poitiers and, some few leagues farther south, the great basilica of Ligugé Abbey.

Because of the perils of Mal Forest, the gate of Clear Water would be barred at sunset and the great dogs loosed from their chains for the night.

Idrun's father was well off for all the taxation, but Idrun was brought up in the usual rough Frankish way—early taught how to use the fishing-rod, the bow and arrows and the axe, early accustomed to climb both tree and mountain, to be unafraid of storms, and to grow as sturdily as a well-rooted apple-tree. The four seasons spoke clearly to him, and he loved the small world around him.

Those were unkindly days for his country. There was a shadowy King of the Franks, and few people in Idrun's neighbourhood knew his name. The real ruler of the land was Duke Charles, nominally Mayor of the Palace, whose constant wars against the Belgics, the Saxons and the savage Slav tribes to the North meant annual musters. None but free-born Franks were called to serve in the army. Berno's labourers were all freed slaves of alien birth, and he did not have to send anyone to the muster at Tours or Poitiers, but the Count's men came to Clear Water and demanded money, cattle, horses and victuals, and Berno gnashed his teeth at the demands but he had to meet them.

Clear Water was more or less self-contained because of its

isolation. Few pilgrims or other travellers passed that way, but life at the steading beat to such a high pulse that there was no monotony. Once outside the gate, anyone could meet either adventure or peril. The lovely, wild country to the north of Poitiers afforded enough scope for both. There were brigands, thieves, wild beasts. Idrun was quite small when one softly golden morning in late September when they were on their way to Mass, a huge wolf sprang out from the undergrowth, crouched and prepared to spring again, its eyes glinting. In less than an instant Berno had his big axe between his hands, stepped back a little,

aimed true so that the blow cleft the wolf's head in two, and the great body rolled down to the track and lay still. The servants missed Mass that Sunday—so busy were they dragging the huge carcass to the manor. The flesh was given to the dogs, the skin, carefully dried, handed over to the sewing-women to be lined with wool and turned into winter coverlets, and most of the bones, very carefully cleaned, were put aside for knife handles and needles. All waste was considered sinful at Clear Water.

That day, Idrun gave up trying to say his prayers at Mass. He thought of the terrible wolf, the upraised axe gleaming in his father's hands, and he felt proud, excited, and also frightened.

A little later when he was barely eight, Berno got the smith at the forge below the chapel to make a small axe, and taught Idrun how to hold it with both hands, to step back and to strike, a block of wood being the target.

Idrun aimed wrong. The axe whistled and glanced off the wood. He let it go and it got embedded in the grass.

'See,' said Berno, 'had you not stepped back and leant your body forward, the axe would have fallen on your foot. And you did not hold it properly either. An axe is a weapon and not a spoon. Grip it, I tell you, and never mind if it hurts your wrists. You'll get used to it, lad.'

Idrun did, but he never dared tell his father that Clear Water

meant much more to him than the thick-walled house, its surroundings, the care needed to look after oxen, poultry, bean fields
and fruit-trees. It was a world gorgeously painted through all the
four seasons, a song and a secret. Below the grim forest on the way
to Poitiers, where they went three or four times a year, lay the
shining heart of the secret: at Ligugé Abbey, where the librarian,
Idrun's friend from the beginning, sat reading and writing. . . .

The morning of the broken crock led to a day of major and
minor disasters. One of the serving-women broke three needles—
one after another. A young dairy-maid stumbled on a stone and
dropped a basketful of eggs; she wept over the yellow-stained
shells, but her tears did not prevent Malina, the foreman's hot-
tempered wife, from beating her. Some animal, seen by nobody,
managed to find its way in and devoured four fowls, leaving a
mess of orange and white feathers all over a newly planted bed of
celery. In the house, the fire, having sulked all the morning,
suddenly blazed up and the dinner porridge was burned. Berno
was out, and Aldis, having rated the two cooks, sent them out of
the hall, and herself started fussing about the dinner, boiling large
pieces of bacon and stirring the batter for the pancakes. Malina
shuffled up the hall and started complaining about the dairymaid's
clumsiness, but Aldis did not listen.

'Don't you see I am busy? The master must not be kept waiting
for a meal.'

'Well, mistress, it is lucky that we happened to have enough
eggs for the batter,' retorted Malina, and shuffled away to find
something else to grumble about. Fault-finding was meat and
drink to that tall, fat woman.

But Berno did not come for his dinner. Idrun and all the
servants ate their allotted portions in silence. Aldis did not touch
hers. She ordered the meal to be put into flat-lidded platters and
covered with hot ashes. So anxious was she that she never noticed
Idrun crouching by the open door and idly trying to mend a
fishing-rod.

Berno did not come till late in the afternoon, his face grim, his mouth stern, and his clothes muddy. Aldis, waving a servant aside, herself set the meal on a trencher, brought a wooden dish of apples and nuts, and poured out the mead into a large horn cup. Berno cut off a piece of bacon, pushed the trencher away, looked at Idrun, now gone into the farthest corner, and thundered:

'What's the matter with your hand?'

Idrun blushed a wild red. Aldis said calmly, 'He cut it rather badly, and I put some ointment on.'

'I won't have him pampered,' Berno shouted, bit into an apple, and emptied the horn cup. 'He should have sucked it and then put some grass on it. Ointment indeed! I want some bread, wife, and more mead, too.'

Idrun stole out of the house. Aldis fetched the loaf and refilled the horn cup. She had not asked a single question. Berno finished the apple, chewed some bread, and then said thickly:

'Wife, I seem to have got into trouble—but I mean to get clear of it, Our Lady and St Martin helping me.'

Aldis waited. So did Idrun outside the door.

'My father and his father were such true friends of Ligugé Abbey,' began Berno, 'and I have been, too. Now it is all changed—all because of that new prior they've got, and the Abbot does not care. He's got his nose buried in his books. Ah, wife, learning leads to no good.'

Idrun heard and shivered for all the sunlight felt warm to the flesh. Berno struck the table with a clenched fist.

'I had meant to go to Troissant this morning and talk to Turgot, as I told you, all about those tax difficulties. Turgot has a far better head than I have—'

'Was he away from home?' Aldis ventured to ask and Berno shouted:

'Am I telling you what happened or is it the other way round? Gracious heavens! There is not a woman born but she is sister to a magpie. Now, then, I was hardly out of the gate before Libun, the swineherd, met me, and he was in tears, wife—'

Berno paused for some more mead. Aldis had enough temerity to murmur almost under her breath: 'Wolves, husband?'

Berno's laughter rang angry.

'Well, you might call them wolves—in sheep's clothing. As usual Libun had taken the pigs to the oak coppice, and he hardly settled himself down under a tree when two Ligugé monks appeared—not on foot either—in a cart drawn by an ox. The coppice belonged to the Abbey, they told Libun. And what could the man do? They caught two pigs, trussed them up, and drove away.'

'Certainly the oak coppice does not belong to the Abbey.' Aldis's voice shook.

'That is not the end of it,' Berno went on gloomily. 'Libun had enough sense to round up the pigs out of the coppice and to drive them into the orchard here. And no sooner had I heard his tale than I met Grifo, his face as black as thunder. He had been down to the Silver Lake and seen two other monks take the pike and the carp my men had got. Grifo said to the monks that he was my foreman, and they laughed at him and drove away, our fish in the cart! Robbers, that is what they are all because of Prior Simeon, but I mean to get even with him—'

'Husband, surely the Silver Lake is not on the Abbey lands?'

'Of course it is not. How could it be? Such a distance! Those four monks must have spent a night at their hospice at Poitiers before they got here. It is all the work of that nasty rat-faced Prior Simeon, and all because I told him I could not afford to give silken hangings and a gold chalice to them, taxes being as high as they are, and I have got Sir Martin to think of too—one can't let one's parish priest starve, can one?'

Aldis said calmly, 'We can send our pigs elsewhere, husband, and there are good fish in the Clain. In a few days we'll be going to Poitiers, and you will ride on south to the Abbey and put it all straight.'

'Yes, wife, if the old Prior Peter were there, God rest his kindly soul'—and Berno crossed himself—'but this Simeon would rob his own mother of her last copper piece. Oh, yes, we'll go to Ligugé. Later, I'll ride to Troissant—I think Turgot knows of a good lawyer at Tours.'

Aldis said shakily:

'Husband, you don't mean that you are going to the courts?'

'And what else is there to do? The Silver Lake is mine, and for three generations we have had the pannage rights in the oak coppice. If I never set foot in the Abbey again, I'll teach that cheat of a prior that he can't rob me—'

Idrun could listen no more. Tears nearly choking him, he ran across the yard and found Gunto in one of the outbuildings busily cutting wood for kindling.

'There is so much trouble, Gunto,' he began, and the other nodded.

'I know. I heard my people talking of it. The monks took the nets as well as the fish.'

'The Silver Lake is ours,' cried Idrun, 'but we can't quarrel with Ligugé, can we?'

Gunto shrugged.

'My father means to go to law.'

'Waste of money,' his friend said. 'The monks will have their way. They always do.'

Idrun cupped his chin in both hands.

'Gunto, I couldn't bear to have my father quarrelling with Ligugé.'

Gunto laid down his knife, whistled, and asked:

'When did it all start, Idrun?'

There was a pause. Idrun was searching for words and they were not easy to come to his tongue. He sat on the ground, his legs crossed, his hands clenched, and Gunto wondered at the curious light in his friend's eyes.

'I think,' Idrun began slowly, 'it happened two or three summers ago when my father first took me down to the Abbey. When we got there, nobody took the least notice of me except a bent-shouldered little monk who took me by the hand and led me down the cloister—'

Idrun paused. Gunto did not interrupt.

'And there, to the left, was a room—full of parchments and books and ink-horns. . . . Such a small room, Gunto. . . . It was the library, and the monk was Dom Defensor, the librarian. When he began talking of books, it was just like one window opening after another. He showed me some of his own script and I looked at it, and I knew I was blind, and I wanted to stop being blind, Gunto. . . . That was all. . . .'

The other nodded, picked up his knife, and said again:

'But the monks will always have their own way. . . . Idrun, do you want to join them?'

'Never.'

'That is all right then,' muttered Gunto.

It was not all right for Idrun. The sun set and the gate was closed. The serving folk, having supped, made for their straw pallets in the hall and elsewhere. Berno and Aldis mounted to their room. Idrun lay in his corner. He dared not cry—much though he wanted to. He heard his father's snore. He heard an owl hoot. He heard an ox stamping up and down in the nearest stable. He thought his misery would keep him awake, but he fell asleep soon enough.

II

A Storm Within Tranquillity

The narrow long room had no windows, but ample light came through a wide door, always left open by day, which gave out into the cloister, one of the arches being just opposite. Beyond lay the great green expanse of garth with a crude stone cross rising in the centre.

The room had no furniture save for a low, sloping lectern, a stool and a narrow bench littered with inkhorns, sheets of parchment and styles. On the flagged floor lay a straw pallet, and the three walls were covered with shelves affording space for countless manuscripts both bound and unbound, and slim papyrus rolls.

The monk's thin shoulders were bent as he sat on the stool, peering at a sheet of parchment spread on the lectern. His hands, the colour of old ivory, held the parchment in the manner of a lover. To Dom Defensor, the librarian of Ligugé, books meant everything, and the room was his kingdom. He raised his head and glanced towards a corner where several sheets of parchment lay rather untidily. He longed to finish his anthology, but Duke Charles had ordered a psalter. Now it was finished except for a capital in the left-hand corner. It was a dove, carrying a flowering branch in its beak, and Dom Defensor was not sure about it. The branch was traced delicately enough but not yet painted.

He muttered under his breath, 'I suppose it should be an olive branch, but those trees don't grow in our country and I would not know what colour to use, and the buds of apple blossom are coral pink. Oh, dear, I haven't got the right paint, and that means I've got to beg it of Dom Placid, and he'll be as cross as ever. He won't grudge it to me—but the questions he'll ask! And today being Friday, he'll be hungry too. . . . Oh, dear, oh, dear. . . .'

The librarian got up, laid the unfinished sheet on the top shelf, turned and stared at the sunlit garth, and his thin, line-grooved face broke into a smile. Friday, and his dear little friend would be coming to Ligugé within a few days.

Dom Defensor turned. Almost he imagined Idrun's slim body seated on the straw pallet, his red-stockinged legs crossed, his face shining with curiosity and eagerness as his eyes flew from shelf to shelf.

'And what is this, Dom Defensor?'

'Gregory's book of sermons—'

'Who was he?'

'A pope, and a very good one. He loved Frankland.'

'Will he ever come here?'

'Son, he died more than a hundred years ago.'

'What a pity,' sighed Idrun.

And here Dom Defensor remembered the first occasion when the boy said he wanted to learn his letters. Was it two years ago? The monk could not be sure. He had just begun the chapter on Friendship in his anthology and Idrun did not interrupt him. He crept towards the pallet, sat down, watched and waited until the sheet of parchment was ended; Dom Defensor put his style into one of the many inkhorns, and turned round smiling.

'You have very good manners, lad.'

Idrun blushed and stammered:

'Is it your own book you are at?'

'Not quite,' murmured the monk, and added, 'I'll tell you all about it when it is finished.'

The boy's face lit up. His eyes looked as though a small star had a home in each. He said very slowly: 'I want to learn . . . I want to read your books . . . I want to write. Could you—' he gulped. 'Could you teach me?'

'I must ask the Abbot—' Dom Defensor was gentle—'but before I do, lad, you must ask your father.'

The starry look vanished.

'That would be no use. I have heard him say that book-learning should be left to the monks and clergy.'

Dom Defensor reflected.

'I suggest then that you wait. God can do miracles. An opportunity may come your way. What are you now? Eight? Nine? Lad, it is never too late to begin. I was nearly twenty when I came to Ligugé, a fisherman's son, and I knew no letters—'

That happened about two years ago, and someone passing in the cloister must have overheard them. Dom Defensor never knew who it was, but before the two years were over, Berno came to the Abbey and, reining his temper as best he could, told the Abbot that he would never permit his son to learn his letters.

'He'll have Clear Water once I have gone! What time would he have to mess with old parchments? Or is it that you are out to catch him into your net, turn him into a monk, and add my ancestral steading to your possessions?'

Anyone else would have turned such words into an occasion for a vehement quarrel, but people could no more quarrel with Abbot Ursin than ride to the moon. He stroked his long white beard before replying:

'Turn Idrun into a monk? Certainly not. He has no call for such a life, and his duty is clear. Teach him his letters? My good friend, nobody would do it unless you gave your consent—'

'And I shall never give it.'

'Then the matter is settled,' said the old man, and invited Berno to have a cup of wine and some barley wafers.

On the next visit, Idrun accompanied his father to Ligugé. The boy looked sad and murmured that things were as they had been. It was obvious that Berno had told him nothing of the tempestuous scene in the Abbot's lodgings, and Dom Defensor kept silent in his turn.

Here he remembered that the Clear Water people would be riding to Poitiers within a few days. As usual, the librarian said a short prayer asking for a miracle to happen.

'Goodness—' he struck his breast—'here I am wasting my time, and Dom Placid is sure to waste more of it.'

The illuminator's workshop was right across the garth, behind the south-west cloister, close to the great gates, and the librarian hurried towards it.

He never had his paint that day. He was almost by the workshop when an unaccustomed tumult by the gates drew him on past the workshop, his face reflecting curiosity more than dismay.

'Such a noise at Ligugé,' he muttered. 'Most unseemly. . . .'

About the middle of the fourth century a young man, called Martin, having passed a few thick forests, reached the broad valley of the Clain. About six miles south of Poitiers he came to a very wild spot, with the grim rocky summits of the Smarves Mountains looming to the east. The spot fully answered his needs, and he decided to build a hermit's hut there. Soon enough Martin's reputation began spreading far and wide: his love of silence, his kindliness to man and beast, his gift of prayer, all these drew others to join him. Huts multiplied, and one of them became a chapel. The men fished in the Clain, and wild berries and roots summed up their diet.

By the beginning of the fifth century that huddle of roughly timbered huts became the great monastery of Ligugé. Its monks had a hospice at Poitiers. The Abbey was wholly self-sustaining. Nothing except salt, spices, wine and olive oil was ever bought at any market. Two or three farms outside the walls were worked by the monks. Within, row after row of workshops spoke of a bee-hive activity. They worked in leather, wood, silver and gold; they obtained the King's permission to strike coins, and their money was legal tender throughout the country. They built the magnificent basilica with their own hands, and their labour and genius went to the making of an interior so exquisite that chroniclers wrote about it.

Pilgrims came in their hundreds—from kings and queens down to humble folk. The founder's great tomb was away to the North at Tours: Martin, the humble hermit, had died there as its bishop. But Ligugé, the very first religious foundation in Frankland, kept its treasures jealously. Foremost among them was the Chapel of the Miracle built on the spot where St Martin, having prayed most earnestly over a young man's body, had restored it to life. Then there was the little bell, once used by him to summon his brothers to prayer and to meals. In Idrun's day, no hands ever touched it; it was supposed to ring of itself, and was believed to quieten a storm and to silence thunder.

To Idrun, however, the shrines and richly begemmed relics of Ligugé meant little enough. From the very first visit he was drawn to the library, and Dom Defensor's readily given friendship set the boy's heart aflame with the passion for learning.

In 730 the head of Ligugé was one Ursin, so learned a man that his name had winged all over Europe. Buried in his parchments, writing books and reading, Abbot Ursin left the government of the house to his prior, one Dom Peter, whom the monks called

'Prior Honey'—so sweet his manner, so kindly his behaviour. Dom Peter by no means neglected his work: he looked into all things, and was friends with all. He did not consider that Ligugé lacked anything, and never advised his abbot to start a lawsuit, an expensive occupation which greatly delighted most of the religious houses at the time. The lawyers at Poitiers, who looked after Ligugé's interests, used to say that if other abbeys and priories brought them as little business as Ligugé, they would have to beg for their bread.

But Dom Peter died very suddenly in 728. It was for Abbot Ursin to choose a prior, and the choice brought to an end much of the kindly climate at Ligugé. Ursin's name was indeed famous in the world of letters. In practical details he was about as good as a newly hatched chick. Someone having said to him, 'There is Dom Simeon. He'll make a good prior,' Ursin chose Dom Simeon.

The new prior was a remote cousin to Duke Charles and he never forgot it. His father kept an apothecary's shop at Tours. His mother came of a sturdy farmer's stock. Dom Simeon, when looking at a silver coin, imagined it turned to gold. His activity would have made a busy bee seem idle by comparison. He knew his letters only too well. It pleased him greatly to bury his flat stubby nose in old parchments, and to discover that here and there the rights of Ligugé had been slighted, ignored, or left to lapse. There was not a meadow, a wood, or a reach of some river but Prior Simeon discovered that Ligugé had a lien on it. For all the multitude of his daily jobs, Prior Simeon always found time to bury himself in parchments so old they all but crumbled at the touch. The lawyers at Poitiers were only too pleased at such a harvest of golden apples falling to their share. The monks were not. They thought the Abbey possessions were big enough without being enlarged by virtue of a few sentences on a charter so old that few could decipher it.

And they had other grievances. Prior Simeon decided that the surplus of any harvest yield was to be sold at the Poitiers market instead of being added to the usual dole for the poor in the neighbourhood. That, the monks murmured among themselves, led to much hostility of the common folk. And Ligugé had never been known for meanness, nor had anyone ever heard of a prior dining and supping by himself, the food being brought from the Abbot's kitchen. The monks, swallowing thin and unseasoned broth, chewing equally tasteless roach, dace and pike, and struggling with stale barley bread, felt that they were treated to a series of penances they had not deserved.

Yet Prior Simeon had been elected by the Abbot and there seemed nothing for them to do. A neighbouring farmer or two, dispossessed of a meadow or a wood, would carry a vehement protest to the Abbey, but the Prior was capable of finding proofs where none existed. 'That meadow,' he would say, 'was given to us by none other than King Dagobert himself. Go to Poitiers and our lawyers will show you the charter. Or else go to the Count's court and prove your case.'

The farmers heard, swore, and turned away. Illiterate, they knew that a look at any charter would be waste of time. Shrewd, they knew that the Count's court would never decide in their favour.

Prior Simeon was of middle height and rather stout. His cheeks were rosy and his beard always carefully combed. He never shouted or lost his temper. He always spoke in even and honeyed accents, which did not deceive many of his listeners.

But, having plunged Ligugé into a vortex of small and irritating economies, Prior Simeon was careful enough never to grudge what materials they needed to Placid, Defensor and a few others. Defensor never went short of parchment, or Placid of paint. And the Prior knew that those men were not gossip-mongers: they never carried grievances past the Abbot's door, and Ursin, satisfied that his house was wholly out of debt, asked for no more.

'What a noise!' muttered Defensor and drew near the great gates.

What he saw was something out of the ordinary monastic rut: two carts, one laden with fish still in their nets, the other carrying two big pigs, both trussed up and both extremely vocal. Each cart, drawn by two oxen, held two obviously embarrassed monks. The shouting, however, did not come from them. It was the cellarer, a mountain of a man, and two or three labourers in rough brown smocks. The cellarer was screaming at the monks. The labourers were shouting at the cellarer, and the pigs were venting their misery and anger on everybody.

'Whatever made you stay at the hospice in Poitiers?' thundered the cellarer at the cart drivers. 'You should have driven straight back.'

'Yes—and through the Mal Forest in the dark,' muttered the youngest of the four monks. 'The Prior never told us to get back the same day.'

'And see the trouble you've brought.'

'The monks should not thieve,' shouted one of the labourers. 'It's a good thing our master sent us to Poitiers yesterday. Even the scullion at the Golden Grape knew where the fish and the pigs came from.'

The cellarer stared.

'And who may you be?' he demanded in a voice as cold as ice.

'We are men from Troissant down in the valley,' retorted one of the men. 'And our master, Turgot, is a great friend of Clear Water! So we knew the marks on the fishing-nets. The Silver Lake is nowhere near your Abbey properties, and we guessed the pigs came from there too—'

Dom Defensor heard and stiffened. The cellarer's face went copper-red and he clenched his fist. The labourers, conscious that they had scored a point, took to shouting all the louder, the pigs accompanying them. Into the turmoil broke the Prior's voice:

'Drive in,' he said to the four monks. 'Where is the porter? Have the gates closed at once and if these ruffians go on making trouble, I'll have them beaten hard. From Troissant, are they?'

As though at a movement of a magician's wand, the two carts drove through. The porter and an embarrassed pink-faced novice closed the heavy gates. The men from Troissant kept on their shouting for a while, but nobody answered them. The cellarer, mopping his forehead, moved away. So did Prior Simeon and Dom Defensor, his hands shaking, his voice unsteady.

'The Silver Lake does not belong to us,' he stuttered, 'and where have those pigs come from?'

'None of your business.' Prior Simeon's smile made the remark all the more offensive. 'And don't talk to me about any Silver Lake. That piece of water is called Mondulat, and it is ours—'

'Since when?' insisted Dom Defensor. 'The folk at Clear Water have been our friends for generations.'

Prior Simeon spoke silkenly.

'Go to the library, brother, and I'll bring you proofs to convince you—'

'The library?' echoed Dom Defensor. 'Indeed no,' and he turned to the left, towards the garth, past the cloister into a small enclosed garden. At the end of it an open stone stairway led to Abbot Ursin's lodgings.

But Dom Defensor was unlucky. At the very door, an elderly brother, who looked after Ursin, stopped him. The Abbot would be engaged till after dinner, he told Dom Defensor.

'It is a rare manuscript lent us by the librarian of St Médard,' explained the monk. 'The Abbot told me not to interrupt him. The messenger from St Médard is coming to fetch it just before dinner.'

His heart heavy, his mind still enflamed with indignation, Dom Defensor went back to the library. The Prior must be told that Ligugé should not make enemies on its right hand and on its left. The Clear Water folk had been friendly for generations, and never a will did they make but the Abbey was remembered in a most generous way.

Dom Defensor started crossing the great garth. Pink-breasted pigeons were making their music all along the eaves of the east cloister; the grass was gaily threaded with tiny red-hearted daisies. Away to his left the great spire of the basilica raised its golden beauty to a cloudless sky. It was a day for wonder and gratitude. But Dom Defensor felt cold and saw none of the beauty.

He remembered that the Clear Water people were expected

within a few days on their customary visit. He had looked forward to seeing Idrun again. He had meant to tell him all about the book now finished. Dom Defensor also hoped to see Berno alone for a few minutes and to win his consent for Idrun to learn his letters.

Now all these hopes were shrivelled as dead leaves tossed by the late autumn winds. Dom Defensor had known Berno for years. The man's temper would never forget or forgive such an injustice. . . .

The monk sighed as he reached the east cloister, and then stopped and winced as though a horsefly had stung him.

In the doorway of the library stood the Prior, a tattered piece of parchment in his hands and a peculiar smile on his lips.

'So you have been to the Abbot's lodgings, brother,' he said politely. 'Yet you are no raw novice. You know that you should have asked your Prior's permission before you went.'

Dom Defensor said nothing.

'I'll overlook it for once,' Prior Simeon went on, 'all the more so since I know the Abbot was not to see anyone this morning.'

He turned into the library, Dom Defensor following him. Slowly, almost too slowly, the Prior laid the tattered piece of parchment on the lectern and smoothed it out.

'Here is your proof,' he said softly, 'since after the Abbot, you are the most learned member of our community, it is only right that you should see it.'

Dom Defensor stooped over the lectern.

'What date do you give this charter?' he asked.

'503,' answered Prior Simeon, 'in King Clovis's reign. See his sign manual at the bottom of the sheet? To think that for more than two hundred years those people at Clear Water should have fished in the lake which did not belong to them and fattened their pigs on acorns in our woods.'

Dom Defensor peered more closely. His voice rang cold:

'I can see no mention of the Silver Lake in the charter—'

'Of course not. That is the name coined by common folk in the neighbourhood. The proper name of the lake is Mondulat, and, as you see, it comes seven times.'

The other made no reply. He picked up the parchment and carried it to the open doorway to examine it properly. Behind him, the Prior settled down on the stool and glanced at the little chest near the lectern. 'I must tell the cellarer not to give wax candles to Dom Defensor,' he thought. 'Tallow is good enough.'

Here he was startled by the librarian's sudden movement. So briskly did he turn that a wood-bound volume, caught by a sleeve of the habit, clattered on the stone floor. Dom Defensor put the parchment back on the lectern. His sunken eyes were ablaze, his mouth trembled.

'It is a fake.'

'What?' The Prior rose from the stool.

'It is a fake,' repeated the librarian. 'You should never have shown it to me, Dom Simeon. I know the Merovingian script well enough and I know their spelling, too. Not a single mistake in the whole of the text! This is no more King Clovis's sign manual than mine.' Dom Defensor laid a shaking hand on the parchment.

Quick as lightning, the Prior stretched out an arm, hit the librarian across the face, and regained possession of the parchment.

'That for your insolence,' he panted. 'Do you think your learning will be of use to you when I send you out into the woods to work under a swineherd? You are too proud for a monk, brother—'

'The Abbot shall hear of it,' murmured Dom Defensor, 'and even if tending our pigs I'll still be able to recite Fortunatus's poetry.'

'The Abbot trusts me in all things,' replied the Prior and left the cell.

Dom Defensor sank down on the stool and hid his flaming face in both hands. The Prior's violence and threats had meant little enough. The librarian knew that the clumsily forged charter would never be shown to Abbot Ursin. A scholar of his mettle would reject it at a glance. But the parchment would go to the lawyers at Poitiers, those shifty, cunning men, who would make a copy of it and swear to that copy being taken from a genuine original. That, as Defensor knew but too well, meant a case for the courts. The Prior had had too many of them, and always won.

'Oh, not Clear Water, not Clear Water, not my poor little Idrun,' thought the librarian.

It was a heavy day indeed. Bells rang, and he obeyed their summons mechanically. He followed the other brethren into the frater and had no idea what he was given for dinner. Silence being the rule during all meals, Dom Defensor was left alone with his thoughts. Somehow the hours crept on. He did not see the Prior again. The Vespers over, Dom Defensor turned back to the east cloister when a monk from their hospice at Poitiers stopped him.

'They are not coming, brother,' he whispered.

'Who are not coming?'

'The folk from Clear Water . . . I can't make anything out of the story, but Berno seems to have quarrelled with us. You know, he always brings us a few pelts. Well, his men were seen at the Golden Grape offering the pelts to a merchant from Chalon. Good pelts they were too—'

'What do pelts matter?' murmured Dom Defensor and vanished into the library.

He was determined to go to the Abbot the very next morning and to tell him that the fair name of Ligugé should not be stained by faked records. Such was his plain duty but, as he groped his way to the dorter above the cloister, Dom Defensor's mind was one big ache for Idrun.

'Shall I ever see him again?' wondered the monk. 'He was such a light on the darkest wintry day—'

III

Thickening Shadows

The evening of that disastrous day closed upon Clear Water, all its
people lost in a bog of bewilderment and anger. Two pigs and a
catch of pike and carp meant little enough as such. But the insult
to their master loomed like a huge blue-black cloud on their sky.
From times immemorial Clear Water had fished in the Silver Lake
and pastured its pigs in the oak coppice. If those shaven heads at
Ligugé thought they had a right to the lake and the little wood,
they should have sent a messenger with a proper piece of writing.
It did not matter that the master could not read: Sir Martin would
have done it for him.

'Haven't we got enough brigands on roads and in woods?'
grumbled Berno's folk when, the day's last task done, they washed
their hands in the trough at a corner of the yard and made for the
hall to eat their supper.

It was no merry meal. Everybody noticed that the master barely
touched his food and the mistress's face was pale and her eyes red-
rimmed. The last mouthful eaten, Berno did not invite anyone to
give them a song. Heavy, his face flushed with anger, he rose from
the table, and Aldis followed him up the stairway into their room.
Idrun, watching the serving-women clear the table and the floor,
snatched at an apple and bit into it savagely. His mind was all in a
muddle. It seemed unthinkable that Ligugé and Clear Water
should quarrel. . . . He looked about for Gunto, but Gunto had
been ordered out of the hall by his father, Grifo, almost before the
meal was over. There seemed nothing for Idrun to do except to
grope to his pallet at the foot of the stairway. So airless was it there
that he tiptoed across the hall to the opened door, and the sweet
breath of an April night eased him somewhat.

He fell asleep to dream about his father riding to Ligugé to offer battle. He woke, said a prayer, and tried to reassure himself that all would be well. They would journey south within a few days. His father would lay his complaint before Abbot Ursin, and everything would be as peaceful as it had been for years and years.

Grifo, being the foreman, had a one-roomed shack of his own cheek-by-jowl to the store-rooms at the back of the house. He had eaten no supper in the hall, and Malina bustled about, getting bread, bacon and beer.

'Eat, husband,' she urged him in her hoarse voice. 'You can't meet trouble on an empty stomach.'

Grifo's calloused hands crumbled some bread. Then he snatched at his horn cup and emptied it.

'No more beer do you get unless you have some bacon.' Malina leant forward and put the empty cup behind her.

Grifo stared at her as though she were a stranger, but he pulled his knife out of the belt, hacked at the bacon, and began munching. Malina crossed her huge red arms, sat down on a trestle, and waited.

'Where's the lad?' Grifo asked thickly, and Malina gestured towards a corner.

'An earthquake would not wake him. Now, husband, what is going to happen?'

'Master means to go to law,' said Grifo, 'and that is all I know except that he means to talk it over with Master Turgot.'

'He is away,' said Malina. 'Gone to Tours to see a sick kinsman. I heard one of his men say so to Sir Martin the other day. But, husband, going to law—' She crossed herself. 'How could master do it?'

Grifo shrugged. 'He is bent on doing it. That is all I know.'

'What does the mistress say?'

Grifo shrugged again, and Malina pursed her thick lips.

'He'll never get any justice that way,' she muttered, and Grifo nodded.

'The swineherd and those others,' she gulped, 'what did they say?'

'You know, wife,' Grifo broke in impatiently. 'I have told you all about it. Going to law! And he said to me that if the Count's court were against him, he would find some learned man to take the case to Duke Charles and if necessary to the King.'

'The King,' echoed Malina contemptuously. 'He is just a puppet. Give him enough meat and wine, and he'll ask for no more. I ask you—does anyone ever see him? Even at Poitiers I have met folk who did not even know his name. A little puppet made of straw and hay—with a silly tin crown on his head.'

Grifo frowned. 'That is no way for a Frankish woman to speak of her King,' he snarled at her, but Malina went on:

'There is no other way, husband, and you know it as well as I do. Duke Charles Martel is our King for all nobody has thought of crowning him. But tell me, what is master going to do once he gets to Ligugé?'

Grifo shook his head.

'I don't know, and I think he doesn't either. I am tired, wife. It has been a hard day.'

'It has been the same for all of us,' grumbled Malina and began putting crocks and platters away.

It rained the next day, and the men went to work, rough brown hoods pulled over their heads. Idrun went from one allotted task to another and avoided Gunto. Nobody mentioned the Abbey, and Aldis called out to some of the women to help her pack the presents she would be taking to the ladies of St Cross the very next day: some lengths of home-spun woollen stuff, two small crosses carved by Gunto out of boxwood, jars of special apple preserve, fat leather bottles of rosemary beer, and an exquisite piece of Aldis's own embroidery, the borders picked out in red and blue, and a golden cross in the middle surrounded by sprays of harebells and campion. She had worked at it for more than a year. Now that the women were slowly and carefully wrapping it up in a piece of linen, Aldis turned away and her under lip trembled. It seemed such a pity to carry that gift to the nuns who, no doubt, would have heard all about the unfortunate affair of the Silver Lake.

'And they all stand together,' thought Aldis. 'Perhaps it were better for us not to go.'

She raised her head and saw Malina at the foot of the stairway. 'Yes?' asked Aldis.

'There has been a messenger from Troissant, mistress. Master Turgot won't be back home till the end of the week, the man said.'

Aldis spoke uneasily. 'I'll tell the master after dinner.'

Yet some time before they began the meal, Aldis, standing in the doorway, saw Berno in the yard talking to Grifo. The message from Troissant had been delivered. She heard Berno say:

'Yes, four men to go with your mistress tomorrow, and let them stay at the Golden Grape. I shall expect them back in two or three days. See that the palfrey is saddled for the mistress and she'll need a cart for all the gear she is taking—' He paused, and Grifo ventured:

'Is my son to go with the young master?'

'Idrun is not going,' cut in Berno, 'and none of the men are to go near the Abbey hospice. Is that understood?'

'Yes, master.'

Aldis's eyes clouded with tears. Berno's mind was made up, but did Idrun know? She could not tell. The early morning's silver rain had gone. The pale skies darkened and the wind dropped. Aldis watched her husband make for the stables, and her hands clenched. How could Clear Water quarrel with Ligugé? It was a matter for men, that she knew, but her Idrun worked so hard, he deserved that holiday.... Aldis turned back into the house, unshed tears all but choking her. Was there not enough trouble and discomfort in the world, she thought confusedly, without there being a tumult at Clear Water? She went up the stairway and sent the two serving-women out of her room. She had not seen Idrun about, and wondered if he knew.

When the boy came to dinner, Aldis guessed he did not. Idrun's lips were set in a thin line, but there was no deadness in his eyes. Berno, tired after a hard morning's work, ate in silence and, the meal over, mounted up to his room for the midday rest. Aldis knew that a single question from her would stir him into anger, and for once she found herself with time on her hands. The packing was done, and Berno had seen to the arrangements for her travelling. There stood her embroidery-frame, but Aldis was in no mood for needlework.

The midday silence fell over Clear Water. The skies shone most deceptively blue, but Aldis could sense more rain on the wind. She left the doorway and walked across the yard. There was no sign of Idrun.

Suddenly, from somewhere behind the house, she saw Gunto, and beckoned to him.

'You are not going to Poitiers tomorrow?' she asserted rather than asked.

'No, mistress,' he mumbled and hung his dishevelled head.

'And does Idrun know?'

'My father has forbidden all the men and me, too, to mention it to him, mistress. My father said it was the master's business and not ours, mistress.'

Aldis nodded. 'God be praised for the folks' loyalty,' she thought briefly.

'Were you with Idrun in the morning?'

'Yes, mistress. We were ditching the back end of the kitchen-garden.'

'And Idrun asked no questions?'

'He never spoke at all, mistress.'

'Ah!'

But here Gunto ventured:

'Yet I think he knows, mistress. Just before dinner, when we were washing, he ran off to the stables and—and—'

'And what?'

'He whispered that the master's gear was not there, mistress.'

'Ah! And what did you say?'

Gunto blushed wildly, dug his bare feet into the young grass, and did not answer.

'What did you say?' asked Aldis icily.

'That—that—I knew nothing, mistress.'

'You are lying.' Aldis raised her right arm and struck hard at Gunto's face. 'For the third time, what did you say to my son?'

Gunto's lips never moved. His left cheek burned after the blow. He hung his head.

'I shall tell your father to whip you hard this evening. You are not to come to supper, understand? You may go—'

But at sunset Aldis had good reason to forget her threat: Clear Water had a visitor just before the gates were closed for the night.

It was a pilgrim, a thin, under-sized man with a ravelled reddish beard and small blue eyes. He wore a short brown smock, with a wide grey cloak over it, his feet and legs were bare, and he carried the usual pilgrim's staff, its handle clumsily carved into a cross. Of luggage he had none except for a small woollen pouch tied to a hempen cord which served him as a girdle.

Callers were rare at Clear Water, and a pilgrim was welcome all the more so because of the day's anxieties and uncertainties. Berno greeted the man politely, and Aldis plunged into activity. Serving-women ran here and there at her orders. Hot water, two towels and a comb were brought in at once. Extra dishes for supper were ordered. The long table was set with roasted eggs, some pickled fish, home-made sausage, bread, cheese and beer. Malina brought in a sweet tart and put it in the place of honour in front of Berno's chair.

The pilgrim was hungry. Finishing the fish, he told them he had been to St Denis, and was now on the way south to Poitiers there to pray at the shrine of St Cross.

'Poitiers,' echoed Berno, 'why, my wife is going there at sun-break. You'll travel in good company, my friend. Mal Forest is not a pleasant place for a lonely traveller.'

The pilgrim sighed.

'I have heard of it. It is not the only wood in Frankland to avoid.'

Aldis leaned forward and piled the guest's platter with sausage and cheese.

'You are a true Christian,' he said appreciatively. 'Why, in some places they'd send me packing with a mug of sour milk and a dry crust.'

They all waited politely. At one end of the long table Idrun sat, his head low, an uneaten egg on his platter. So it was true what Gunto had said. His mother would be travelling alone, and Dom Defensor would never know. . . . Here Idrun heard his father's sharp voice.

'Eat your supper, son, and stop looking like a half-slaughtered sheep.'

Idrun swallowed the food he did not want. He kept peering down the length of the hall, but Gunto was not there, and all those present were greedily listening to the visitor. From Poitiers he would make for Vienne, then cross the Alps, stay at Pavia a bit, and winter at Ravenna.

'Come next spring—' his blue eyes were laughing—'I hope to get to Rome. Folks are always kind to a pilgrim—' but here his seamed, weather-beaten face darkened. 'Such a lot of trouble, though, in the world today. I have heard people talk about invasions in such a way you'd think the enemy was at your doorway! Lombardy is quarrelling with the Pope. Byzantium is like a house divided against itself. There are rumours of savages coming from the far North—I don't even know what they are called. And the Saracens in Spain! What will you? Here you live in peace'—he bowed to Berno and Aldis—'but there is famine all round about Orléans, and at St Denis they have cut down the pilgrim's dole.' He sighed. 'Just bean-broth and bread for the pittance! Duke Charles is summoning muster after muster to fight the Saxons and the Slavs. So many a field lies neglected—you can't work the land with women and children.' He sighed again, and raised his head.

'What a guest I am, seasoning your supper with sad stories,' he cried. 'Now when I was trudging out of Tours, my heart was as light as my stomach, and why? Because spring took hold of me and sang of the Lord's Resurrection, and there was a small chapel by the wayside, an old priest serving it. It was near sunset. Ah, he seemed poorer than me for all he had a pig and two or three fowls. He feasted me royally. When I told him all I had heard on my wanderings he said: "Son, a burden and a pigeon's feather are the same weight in God's sight."'

He stopped. The servants cleared and scrubbed the long table. Berno sent for some more mead, and the pilgrim knew they were all expecting a story from him. He had heard one at St Denis about a big bird called Phoenix, which lived in a remote country over the seas.

'It lives for five hundred years. Then it fills its wings with scented herbs and flies to a city far away from its home, there to throw itself into a fire burning within a great marble palace. The day after a worm stirs in the ashes. At sunset that worm turns into a young bird, a fledgling Phoenix, you might say. In about a week it flies back to its old home, and there lives for another five hundred years.'

The serving folk had listened, their mouths wide open. Berno refilled the guest's cup and said approvingly:

'A fine tale, Master Pilgrim.'

'Ah, but there is more to it.' The guest drank some more mead and Aldis asked:

'And what are its colours?'

'The chest is tawny-orange, the beak golden, the tail garnet-red and blue. One wing is dark violet, the other as blue as the June sky. And the crest is as brilliant a green as you see on the emerald in a bishop's ring.'

'You said there was more to it,' Aldis prompted.

'Ah yes, mistress. It comes from a big book they have at St Denis, and a kindly monk explained it to me. The story has a hidden meaning. The two wings stand for the Old Testament and the New. The fire in the marble palace means the holy hill of Calvary, and life stirring in the ashes is our Lord's Resurrection.'

'Ah,' breathed Idrun, 'I have had this story read to me at Ligugé—by Dom Defensor.'

Berno frowned. Aldis seemed embarrassed, and the pilgrim did not look pleased.

'Ah, in that case, it must be like shrivelled leaves to you. I suppose you know why the lion sleeps with his eyes open?'

'No,' muttered Idrun.

'Well, then, this stands for the image of Christ's body upon the Cross even though He was also in heaven with God the Father.'

They all forgot Idrun's untimely interruption and clamoured for more stories. Pleased at having kept their attention, the pilgrim told them about the pelican offering her blood for her young, about a long-necked animal which, by swallowing a snake, would be turned into one, and he also told them of a very precious pink stone in possession of an Eastern ruler. It changed its colour to blue once put on a liar's finger.

'But those people,' added the pilgrim, 'not being Christian, can't see God's judgment in that marvel.'

Aldis nodded.

'There is no end to wonders in God's world,' she murmured.

Yet it was getting late. The women had already prepared some bedding for the guest not far from the opened doorway. One by one, the rushlights were put out. The fir-cones in the fire looked like so many roses shot through with golden light, and the night's quiet fell over Clear Water. In the silence, peopled with shadows, Idrun rose from his pallet and, his bare feet making no sound on the rushes, crept towards the pilgrim's corner.

'Master,' he whispered urgently, 'will you be going to Ligugé after Poitiers?'

The pilgrim muttered sleepily, 'Of course not. I'll be going east to Vienne. Ligugé? No place for pilgrims now with that skinflint of a prior! He'd grudge you a crust, lad . . .' and he turned his face away.

Idrun, lead in his heart, crept back to his pallet.

The sun was just about to set when the party from Clear Water reached Poitiers.

It had not been a very happy journey, and even the pilgrim's songs could do nothing to dispel the shadows. Aldis riding her palfrey, with Malina and two other women behind, could think of nothing but her son whom she had not seen when leaving the steading. The customary hustle and bustle had started some time before daybreak, but Idrun had vanished—and even Grifo could not tell where he had gone. The last bundle put into the cart, Aldis had turned to her husband.

'You can't quarrel with friends,' she had murmured, blood rushing into her cheeks.

'That prior is no friend of mine,' said Berno. 'Once Turgot is back, I'll ride over and ask his advice. There are some parchments in the chest in our room. A good lawyer at Tours will deal with them—and the Count's court will settle the case.'

Sighing, Aldis had said:

'Husband, you will never go to law.'

He would not answer, and, all bewildered, Aldis had thought,

'He will never win the case. . . . To quarrel with Ligugé. . . . It is
unthinkable—all because of two pigs and some fish,' but she had
not dared say so.

So they had started at sun-break, the evidences of spring on their
right hand and on their left. The track widened and narrowed. Far
away to their left, the silver ripple of the Clain now gleamed, now
vanished behind the screen of tall larches. To their right, the range
of the Smarves rose far less forbidding than in winter, a shelf of
bold young green breaking the dark grey stone here and there.
They reached the outskirts of Mal Forest, and went through it, no
beast or brigand disturbing them, and soon they saw the roofs and
spires of Poitiers caught into the dazzle of an April sunset.

At the gateway of St Cross Abbey two of the men dismounted,
and Aldis was startled by the sullenness of their looks. They had had
their instructions: they were to go to the Golden Grape and stay
until their mistress was ready to return to Clear Water, and they
were not to talk to anyone about their master's quarrel with Ligugé.

The bent-shouldered portress welcomed them, her toothless
mouth curved in a smile, and Aldis forced herself to return the
smile. Her women carried in the bundles and she, her embroidery
in her hands, followed the nun to the church where the gift was
laid at the foot of the reliquary of the true Cross. Aldis knelt for a
brief prayer, then rose and followed the portress to the guest-
house where her cousin, Dame Melita, awaited her. The room was
small and scantily furnished, but the leather bed was covered with
sheepskins, there was the luxury of two wax candles on the table,
and a supper of savoury stew, wheaten bread, goat's cheese, and a
dish of apples and nuts. Aldis stopped at the threshold and clenched
her hands. Dame Melita, plump and rosy, came forward and
kissed her on both cheeks.

'It is good to see you, and oh—the presents you have brought.'

Aldis stared about her. 'I think I am hungry,' she said inconse-
quently. 'I believe we did stop for dinner but I could eat nothing,
oh nothing—'

'Then have your supper, cousin,' Dame Melita said sensibly.

Aldis sat down on a bench. The stew smelled good. She dipped the horn spoon into the dish and ate voraciously. Dame Melita, her hands folded in the wide sleeves of her habit, sat down opposite and waited. The stew eaten, she urged her cousin to have some fruit and nuts. Aldis shook her head, but in the end she took an apple and began nibbling at it.

'We are in such trouble, cousin,' Aldis began, and stopped. She could not remember whether Berno had told her to say nothing about Ligugé. She frowned, the apple in her hand, when two nuns appeared in the doorway: Dame Werburga, a learned lady from Northumbria, and Dame Gisla, whose wit was remarkable by its absence. Both bowed to Aldis, and Dame Werburga delivered

herself of a polished little speech of gratitude on the part of the Abbess whose state of health did not allow her to leave her lodgings for a few days.

'Such exquisite embroidery and all the other things.'

Courtesy should have made Aldis ready to make room for the two ladies and to have indulged in a spell of harmless gossip. But she was tired. Her thoughts were all tattered. She bowed to the two nuns and turned to Dame Melita:

'I hope the ladies will forgive me this evening. There is—' she hesitated—'a family matter I must discuss with my cousin.'

Dame Werburga permitted herself something of a shrug. Dame Gisla tittered. But both went.

'That will be all over the house,' said Dame Melita gloomily. 'I know what the trouble is, cousin. The whole of Poitiers has heard of it by now—Ligugé claims a small piece of water and a wood from you. Isn't it so? There's talk about a very old charter—'

'Berno—' Aldis stared at the wooden dish of fruit—'means to take it to court. He is waiting for his friend at Troissant to return from Tours. Berno says he will never employ a lawyer from here.'

Dame Melita pinched her lips.

'No lawyer at Tours will be of use to him, cousin. Ligugé is rich and powerful. They give with one hand and take away with the other. You remember that orchard we had just behind their hospice? It was ours by law—planted on the land bought by the Abbess Radegund. Well, the monks alleged that Radegund's purchase was illegal'—Dame Melita spread her hands—'and our Abbess would rather touch the devil's hand than go to law. So we've lost the orchard.'

Aldis straightened her shoulders.

'Berno would appeal to Duke Charles—'

'Cousin—' Dame Melita spoke urgently—'you and I are well-bred, but to the Duke, Berno is just a farmer, and Berno could not get near the Duke without approaching the Count, and to the Count, Berno is a man who works his land well enough but all his men are freed slaves and can't answer the muster—'

'But we pay all the dues they demand,' said Aldis coldly.

'Ah, yes, but you can't send a single man to fight the Duke's enemies. It is the men they want—not the money. Do tell your husband to be reasonable.'

Aldis's hands began playing with her girdle.

'If that were all,' she murmured, 'but there is Idrun, cousin—'

'Is the lad ill?'

'No, no. But he has a great friend at Ligugé and has set his mind on learning his letters. His father would not hear of it before this trouble—and—and—now it is hopeless—'

'Does Idrun want to be a monk?'

'Oh no! He loves Clear Water so much—'

'Surely, that old priest of yours could be of use?'

Aldis shook her head.

'Sir Martin? He is far too old and besides, Berno won't have Idrun taught, and what is there for me to do?'

Dame Melita sat silent for a few moments.

'A man from Troissant came just before Easter, with the usual offering. It was Dame Gisla's turn at the wicket, and you know what she is like, cousin, don't you?'

'Well?'

'She told us later that man had called Idrun a marvel—with a will like iron. Yes, that is what he said—a lad of iron is Idrun—'

'And his father is a man of iron,' replied Aldis very quietly.

She had been so looking forward to this visit, and now she knew herself disappointed. They had received her as warmly as ever, showered gratitude for the gifts, and Dame Melita, as Aldis knew, had been excused from Compline and evening meditation.

Yet Dame Melita had spoken no words of comfort, and Aldis was unashamedly glad when the bell for Great Silence began ringing up and down the cloisters, and the nun left the guest-house. From an adjoining room Aldis could hear the measured snoring of Malina and her other women. Comfortable bedding had been prepared for herself, but Aldis sat motionless on the bench, both hands propping her chin.

What was happening at Clear Water? Why had Idrun kept away in the morning? Dame Melita had spoken of some charter or other in the monks' possession. Suppose that dreadful prior at Ligugé were to find some other paper and be able to dispossess them of Clear Water entirely! The hands which propped the chin went icy. That would surely kill Berno, and Idrun, a master's son, some day to be himself a master, what would he do? There would be no question of any marriage for him: what girl with a dowry would be allowed to wed a dispossessed beggar? Aldis wept, prayed, and wept by turn.

It was long past midnight when, the candles long since guttered, she groped her way to the bed in the corner. Exhaustion made her sleep, and she dreamt of Idrun going on a long pilgrimage, his feet dusty and bare and his brown smock torn in several places.

IV

Berno Gets Good Advice

Past old St Martin's little chapel, the valley widened a little, then narrowed, and finally vanished in a steep narrow track. A little to the left was the western range of the Smarves Mountains, their grey severity but scantily redeemed by a stunted tree here and there. A few yards away on the right side was a wood of beech and larch. The edges of the track had, as Idrun always thought, music in them: little rills running down to join a stream in the valley, and another, a much wider one, threaded its way across the wood and ran into the waters of the Clain.

Some few hundred yards on you came to a lichened wall on the right side of the track. A great wooden gateway led to a low stone-built house, Troissant, the home of Turgot, Berno's greatest friend.

Tall, broad-shouldered, fair-haired and blue-eyed, Turgot looked every inch a Frank. Troissant was his by inheritance, but few people knew much about him. He sent the men who served him to markets and fairs, and seldom left his home except for the annual business excursion to Tours and an occasional visit to Orléans where his brother was priest. Because the neighbourhood saw Turgot so rarely and knew him so little, all kinds of fantastic stories were woven round about him. Now he was descended from Clovis, the first King of the Franks. Now he was cousin to Duke Charles of the Arnulfing House. Again Turgot and his brother were supposed to have a Frankish nobleman and a Saxon slave for their parents. The last story was particularly fantastic because, by the Frankish law, a free man, marrying a slave, forfeited his own liberty, and no son of his could win preferment in the Church. If any such stories ever came to Turgot's knowledge, he ignored them.

He was a widower with one daughter, Judith, about the same age as Idrun. At first, her mother's nurse, old Wida, had looked after the child and done the cooking, but when Wida had added a pillow to the stew, thinking it to be a piece of pork, Turgot realized that a younger woman was needed at Troissant. The smith's sister, Vorgis, came into the house. She was fairly skilful with her needle but hopeless with Judith who would vanish from the house, stay away for hours, and return, her arms full of herbs, roots, grasses and flowers. All of it would be thrown on the kitchen floor and sorted out by her for purposes known to none but herself. Untidy, her flaxen hair dishevelled, her white smock stained and torn, her bare legs scratched from the ankle to the knee, Judith had a rare wild beauty of her own, the large grey eyes had flecks of green and gold, the firm little chin, the smile which first flowered at the corners of her mouth and then shone in her look, all about the child endeared her to everybody.

Not yet formally betrothed, she knew her father meant her to marry Idrun, whom she had known since babyhood. They met and played often enough, but their encounters were not always fortunate.

'A primrose,' Judith once said to her father, 'is a flower, and that is all. Idrun and I found clumps of them by the bank, and what does he do but crouch and stare at them as though they'd fallen from heaven. So I spat at him for being so stupid.'

'What did he do?' asked Turgot.

'He hit me and I scratched his arm—'

'I should give you a good beating for behaving like a serf's daughter.'

'Ah, but you won't,' laughed Judith and ran away.

She, Vorgis and Wida lived by themselves in a stone lean-to of the house. The rest of Troissant, a spacious hall, with the master's huge bed in the corner, belonged to the men. Unlike Berno, Turgot did not work the land with freed slaves. He would have none but free-born Franks on the steading. This meant that out of twenty men, quite ten would have to join Duke Charles's host for the summer campaign, and not all of them would return in deep autumn, and Turgot would have to ride either to Tours or Bourges, and hire more labourers. He paid a fair wage and treated the men well. Not a corner of Troissant was ever neglected.

One late April afternoon Berno rode up the narrow track, reached Turgot's land, halted at the gateway and sounded his horn. Two men opened to him and, a bulging satchel under his arm, Berno entered the house where Turgot awaited him, a platter of nuts and a jug of rosemary beer on the table. Brief greetings were exchanged, and Berno untied the leather thongs of the satchel.

'From the wife to you,' he said, handing over two finely woven towels and a small stone jar. 'Crimson dye for your tunic,' he explained and dived into the satchel again—'From the wife to Judith.'

There was a finely carved bone comb, a string of pink beads and a pair of red shoes. Turgot, having thanked his friend for the gifts, fingered the little shoes.

'If I could ever make her wear them even to Mass,' he muttered, and did not add that for all he knew the red shoes might be given away to Vorgis's niece.

Berno drank the beer and cracked a few nuts. Turgot asked:

'Has the Count's messenger called at Clear Water?'

'Why, no.'

'Well, he will, my friend. He came here two days ago and my bailiff dealt with the matter. These are difficult days for the country, so fourteen of my men are to join the muster. Surely, you have heard about the Saracens over-running most of Spain?'

Berno shook his head.

'Didn't you go to Poitiers and Ligugé last week?'

Berno avoided the question.

'Yes, come to think of it, I have heard something. But, surely, it needn't concern us. They'll never cross the Pyrenees—'

'You think so, my friend, but the Alps proved no barrier to the Lombards and others,' replied Turgot and refilled Berno's cup.

'But what does the King say?' asked Berno a little indifferently. All those matters did not interest him much. Wars and taxes had become commonplace. He longed to pour out his particular trouble, but courtesy demanded that he should first listen to his host.

Turgot cracked a nut, his thick eyebrows knit in a frown.

'My good friend, what a question to ask! Once I went to Orléans and the yearly assembly was on—in that big field beside the town. There, on a dais, sat a thin, pale young man who wore a golden crown and a gorgeous scarlet mantle, and he spoke slowly, uncertainly—I could not catch a word. I did not wait for the end. I jumped into my saddle, rode into Orléans, and supped with my brother, who could not even tell me the King's name! Poor puppet! He lives somewhere in a manor, and we supply him with a few servants, some clothes, food and wine. He makes a public appearance once a year so that people might remember they have still a King of the Franks. He would not complain if the infidel snatched the bread out of his mouth. He might weep, though—' Turgot shrugged. 'Where is his kingship?'

Berno said stoutly:

'In his descent. He is a Merovingian, and they say that Clovis's father, Merovech ...'

Turgot laughed.

'Someone said they'd seen a pig riding astride a cow. No, my friend, I am the Duke's man.'

'Charles is only Mayor of the Palace.'

'He does not care a rotten twig about titles and dignities,' retorted Turgot. 'But he does care for the country. I am sure that he will be king. But don't let us talk of that any more. I have heard of your trouble with Ligugé.'

Berno leant forward, his face flushed a wild red.

'You have?'

'Well, yes, two of my men went to Poitiers. It's all over the place, you know.'

Berno clenched his fists.

'I stayed at Clear Water when Aldis went. I would not let the boy go either.'

Turgot asked suddenly, 'How many pigs do you keep?'

'I reckon about fifty.'

'And the monks took two.'

Berno nodded and plunged in: 'Now, my friend, I have come over to ask you if you know of an honest lawyer at Tours.'

'What do you want with a lawyer? Help you to recover a couple of pigs and a few fish?'

'Help me to recover my property,' replied Berno with dignity.

Turgot drummed his fingers on the trestle. 'Have you got proofs?'

'There are two or three musty parchments in a chest in our room.'

'Have you read them?'

'No, my friend, you know I have no letters.'

'All I can say is that even if you had a thousand parchments, you would lose the case.'

'Why should I?'

'Because monks always win,' Turgot replied quietly. 'No lawyer would undertake your case, my friend. There is nothing that monasteries and convents like better than litigation. For one or two proofs of yours, they would produce a hundred.'

'But that is not justice,' cried Berno hotly.

'I never said it was.'

'And what would you do if they started claiming Troissant?'

'Troissant is mine—' Turgot's calm manner all but infuriated his friend—'by virtue of documents registered at Poitiers, Tours and Paris, and the most important among them is the charter given to my forebear by our good King Dagobert more than a hundred years ago, and Ligugé knows it. The Silver Lake and the little coppice have no other title than that of custom.'

'So what am I to do?'

Turgot considered.

'In the first place, I'll make you free of my reach of the Clain. That would give you better fish than the Silver Lake. Next, your pigs can have their fill of fodder in a wood lying nearer to Clear Water. Come to think of it, there is a hut for a swineherd, too.'

'You are most generous, but what do I do about Ligugé?'

'I am not generous. I just don't want to see my best friend make a fool of himself. Ligugé? Well, keep away from it for a time. I have never heard of you haunting its doorstep as it were. If you want to argue with them, that skinflint of a prior would get the better of you. As it is, there has been trouble between the monks and my men who poked their noses into what did not concern them. Such a row they made at the Abbey gateway, trying to get the pigs back to you!'

'That,' said Berno, 'shows what people think of the monks.'

'Opinions,' retorted Turgot, 'matter less than a sparrow's feather in legislation—that is—' and he changed the subject. 'How is the lad?'

'Sulking!' Berno bit his underlip. 'You'd think the whole world was smashed for him. You may have heard of his idea—wants to learn, so he tells me, and the librarian at Ligugé is his greatest friend. Well, it'll be a long time before they see me there again, and there's plenty of work for the lad to do without wasting his time on musty parchments. I expect, really, it all began with that

dreadful Prior Simeon: have the boy taught his letters and once I
am gone, get him in as a monk and Clear Water, too. Well, your
advice is not to my liking, friend, but I'll take it.'

'I thought you would,' murmured Turgot. 'You will stay the
night, won't you? The sun is setting. Time they brought the rushlights in.'

Shadows moved up and down the roughly morticed stone
walls. More and more faggots were thrown on the hearth, and the
savoury steam from a big cauldron made Berno remember he had
hardly had any dinner that day. He turned into a corner to wash
his hands and to comb his hair. Turgot's men brought the stew,
the trestles, large chunks of smoked bear ham and bread. The
master and his guest sat side by side. The men sat on the ground,
unsheathed their knives for the ham and the bread, and dipped
their wooden spoons into the stew. They ate in silence, partly out
of courtesy to the visitor, and partly out of fatigue: the day had
been a hard one for them all.

Outside, the first stars gleamed palely across the blue-grey cup
of the sky, and the screech of an owl could be heard now and
again. Within the great flagged hall, the flame of a rushlight
caught now at a sinewy arm bared to the elbow, now at a patch of
dark red on the shoulder of a grey smock. The broad bladed
knives glinted as the men cut up their meat.

Turgot and Berno did little to break the silence. To the latter,
his mind still inflamed by the injustice meted out to him, his
friend's advice seemed at once acceptable and unpalatable. To
Turgot the whole matter was not worth a broken straw, but he
could well see that his friend did not feel at ease and Turgot applied
himself to his supper in silence.

Suddenly, from out of a shadowy corner, Judith appeared, her
best red gown and a grey silk snood emphasizing the importance
of the moment. She bore something very carefully in her cupped
hands, and so lovely did she look that the men stopped chewing
and sat at gaze. But Turgot frowned.

'I never sent for you.'

Judith did not reply. She came nearer the trestle, bowed low to

Berno, and placed an exquisitely made pale green, grey and pink moss cushion by his cup.

'For Idrun, please,' she said shyly and then raised a brown and grubby hand to her mouth.

Berno smiled. 'And he sent you a present—so all is right between you, eh?'

'But nothing has ever been wrong, Master Berno. I could not help spitting and he hit me. I asked for it.' She raised her little head, and the grey silk snood became a silver coronet. She spoke defiantly: 'But it is certain to happen again.'

Turgot broke in: 'Take your beads, girl, and go back to the women. That Vorgis should never have let you put on your feast clothes.'

'I did not ask her, Father. I wanted Master Berno to see that I could be neat sometimes.'

'He has seen you,' retorted her father. 'Now bow, and go.'

Judith vanished into the shadows of the back. The beads she had forgotten to take still glittered in among the crumbs on the table. The men remembered they had not finished their supper, and Berno stared at the cushion of moss.

'Made it herself, did she?'

'Yes,' Turgot growled. 'Oh, dear saints, what a handful of mischief she is! The other day she got badly bitten by a vixen and not a scream out of her. She would be all right were it not for her wildness. Ever heard of a girl climbing a larch to get hold of a scared kitten? Well, not long to wait now, my friend! Your wife and her women will teach Judith how to behave.'

Berno nodded.

The meal was over; the men cleared the trestle, the remnants of ham and bread were given to the dogs, and someone trimmed the rushlights and damped down the fire on the hearth. A very old, bent-shouldered man, his matted white hair falling over his forehead, and his gnarled hands shaking, hobbled nearer the hearth and sprawled there, staring at the embers. Once Turgot's swineherd, Disul was now too old for such work, and spent his days in a quietly busy retirement. Disul was master physician not only for

the entire valley—but farther afield. Bourges and Autun to the
east and south of the Clain had heard of him. His skill with herbs
was great. His spells were powerful. Everyone knew that old Sir
Martin was afraid of him, and Aldis would cross herself at the
mere mention of his name, but he had cured a tiresome ailment of
Malina's by methods known to none but himself.

Turgot leant forward and shouted:

'Disul, look into the future.'

The old man never turned round. But he threw back his head
and huddled his tattered brown cloak closer to his thin body.

'Look into the future, will you?' Turgot cried again.

After a pause, Disul began in a reedy voice:

'I see clouds, master, clouds and clouds, some grey, some purple,
and all of them angry.' Here the reedy voice strengthened, grew
deeper and louder. 'I see a great field covered with strawberries.
Ripe they are but not for eating. And the clouds are turning to
very dark red, and the strawberries grow bigger and bigger, but
no man may eat them—'

He stopped. Turgot said abruptly:

'Disul, I asked you to look into the future, not to bore us with
riddles.'

'I have looked into the future, master,' muttered the old man,
scrambled up to his feet and shuffled out of the hall. Berno crossed
himself. The night was warm but he shivered.

Later, both men in bed, Turgot grumbled:

'I think the old man's wits are failing—clouds and strawberries!
What next!'

'He said they were not for eating,' murmured Berno, crossed
himself again, and fell asleep.

V

How Idrun Came to Win

Idrun had neither expected nor wanted his father to take him to Troissant, but when Berno left Clear Water alone, Idrun felt as sour as though he had eaten a bowlful of unripe bilberries, and the weather answered his mood. It was cold and gusty in the morning and, working with Gunto and a few others at the kitchen-garden hedges, running errands for his mother, and looking for a mislaid knife of his own, Idrun felt that his entire world had turned into a thick grey cloud never to be dispelled. He knew that his mother was against quarrelling with the monks. He also knew that his father's mind was made up, that litigation, whatever the result, was no cheap business and that some of the fields of Clear Water would surely have to be sold. The men Idrun worked with kept silent; Grifo, on being asked an apparently innocent question, merely said that it was the master's business and nobody else's. Gunto had rather obviously been forbidden to mention Ligugé, and Idrun wished he had never been born into a world where nothing happened the way one wished it to happen.

The morning's stint done, he wandered out of the gates, turning southwards along the bank of a narrow stream enamelled by primroses and red-hearted daisies. Idrun passed one clump after another. Then abruptly he turned back and started picking them. His arms laden with the flowers, he hurried back to Clear Water, but even his gift did little, if anything, to brighten Aldis. Her mind wholly absorbed in Troissant, she barely touched her dinner even though Malina and two other women, conscious of their mistress's trouble, had done their best in stuffing a pike with herbs and adding chopped nuts and honey to the pancakes.

When dinner was over, Aldis, instead of taking her needlework into the open air there to enjoy the soothing sunshine and eventually to fall asleep, mounted the stairway to her room. At the top she turned, her face as grey as her gown, and called out to one of the women:

'Fetch the young master to me.'

Idrun went reluctantly enough. Never before had he seen his mother in such a mood, and he felt afraid. Was she troubled about the likelihood of Clear Water being taken from them? He could not tell, but he mounted the stairs very slowly as if each tread increased his own unease.

The low-ceilinged room was airless, the single small window in a corner being closed. Aldis sat on the edge of the bed, her look leaden.

'Draw the curtain behind you,' she told Idrun without looking at him.

He turned and struggled with the heavy leather folds. Now no sunlight from below reached the room. He could not see Aldis's face in the shadows, and sprawled on the floor, his hot hands clenched over his knees.

The silence continued until Idrun wondered if he could endure it another moment, when Aldis spoke:

'Come and sit by me, son.'

His legs almost trembling, Idrun scrambled on to the edge of the bed, and she put a cold hand on his hot wrist.

'Idrun,' she said unexpectedly, 'you did not forget to send the beads to Judith?'

'No,' he muttered.

'And next time she comes to Clear Water or you meet her anywhere, you won't hit her, will you?'

Idrun was bewildered.

'Because,' Aldis went on, 'it is more than ever important that you two should be friends.'

Idrun's bewilderment grew. To him, Judith was just a habit. They had quarrelled and played, fought and made peace ever since their babyhood. He had a vague idea that his parents and Turgot meant them to marry when the right time came. It did not disturb

Idrun particularly. At that time, children would be betrothed by
their parents, property and blood alone were the decisive factors.
Of blood neither Troissant nor Clear Water could boast much
except that both came of good Frankish stock. Thus property
alone would determine the issue. But Idrun could not understand
why his mother wanted to talk about it. What Liguigé had done or
not done had no bearing on the matter. He breathed heavily and
waited.

'There might be no Clear Water for Judith to come to. Your
father is master here and should he decide to quarrel with the
monks, we might lose our land—'

'But Judith will have Troissant,' Idrun muttered, and his
mother's laughter rang bitterly.

'No father is likely to give his only daughter to a dispossessed
stripling,' she told him. 'So you must try hard, my son, and not
displease Master Turgot. Whatever decision your father makes, I
have made my mind to invite Turgot and Judith here very soon,
and have a feast for them. You will have your hair combed and
your feet washed, and I'll find you a present to give Judith, and
you must be polite to her, son, and not lose your temper if she
laughs at something you say.'

Idrun muttered sullenly: 'You'd better invite Disul as well,
Mother. He'll amuse or frighten everybody.'

'Never,' exclaimed Aldis in horror, and in the shadows Idrun
caught the quick movement of her right hand as she crossed herself. 'Have that warlock to a meal in this house? Why, that would
mean Sir Martin coming here with the blessed water and all, and
how do you know if Disul won't put a spell on all the animals
here? Why, I remember how the blacksmith once offended him,
and the blacksmith's cow dropped her calf and died the same
day.'

Idrun chuckled. To talk about old Disul and his misdeeds, both
real and imagined, lightened the air somehow.

'Well, Mother, he's spent all his days at Troissant and Master
Turgot isn't afraid of the spells.'

'Have you ever seen the old man at Mass?' demanded Aldis.

'He is so old—his legs would not carry him so far.'

'He was not always old,' retorted Aldis, 'and even now his legs can carry him as far as that wood between us and Troissant, and he is said to pray to an idol inside a thorn tree.'

Idrun might have said that he knew all about it, the carefully crossed twigs on the ground, the little fire, the incantations in a tongue no living Frank could understand. Idrun knew of such things because Judith had told him, her eyes starry with excitement, and now he kept silent because he did not wish his mother to speak of Judith again.

'Yes, a little feast,' said Aldis, the housewifely quality in her gaining over the piety. 'I have brought some spices from Poitiers, and Malina can make gingerbread. You are so clever with your bow and arrows, son, you and Gunto together can get enough pigeons for a good big pie. The women will wash the towels and napkins. Platters and cups must be polished. There is an unbroached barrel of whortleberry beer. Ah,' she sighed, a wave of contentment suddenly colouring her horizon, 'Clear Water is not a villein's hut, my son.'

Idrun's own mood lightened. However boring it would be to get his hair combed properly, the plans for the feast were certainly doing good to his mother. Even in the dim light he could see the leaden look vanish from her eyes. Good food, sweet scented rushes underfoot, clean linen, burnished trenchers and cups, of such she thought and was filled with pride and satisfaction. Idrun ventured shyly:

'I brought you some wild flowers in the morning, Mother, but you were—busy.'

'I want them,' Aldis cried and stood up. 'Let me just wash my face, son, and I'll come down and take my work to the orchard— you know—under the old pear-tree. Pull back the curtain as you go, will you?'

Idrun nodded. He ran down the stairs and found his bunch of primroses stuck into a dirty crock in the hall, washed the crock, filled it up with fresh water, and ran to the orchard, something like hope stirring in him.

The men and women at Clear Water took heart when they saw their mistress appear at supper, a clean white veil on her head. Aldis enjoyed her food, praising Malina and others for the well-seasoned broth and the grilled carp. She begged one of the men to sing a song and when the rushlights went dim and the clear dark blue night fell over Clear Water, not a man or a woman in Berno's service but praised their Maker for giving them such a pleasant lot. But they were also curious and, with Aldis gone up to her chamber, they crowded round Grifo and Malina.

'Has there been a message from Poitiers?'

'Will the Silver Lake be given back to the master?'

'Have the monks repented of their mischief?'

'Do our pigs go back to the oak coppice?'

Malina, her lips pursed, went out, leaving her husband to deal with that shower of questions. Grifo, having first cuffed his son for stepping on a hound's tail, gave no answers at all.

'The young master wants to sleep,' he told them. 'The master will be home for dinner tomorrow. Be off, all of you.'

Idrun lay on his pallet by the open door, the sweet breaths of an April night caressing his face. It grew chilly, and he drew the thick woollen coverlet closer round his naked body. He could see the trees in the yard, the shape of each at once mysterious and familiar. Horses champed now and again, a pig's snort came from the back of the house, and the owls in the neighbouring wood started talking one to another, and every sound seemed not to disturb but to deepen the stillness of the night. Idrun fell asleep soon enough, to dream of Dom Defensor, primroses, his mother's pleasure in the coming feast, pigeons, and a light-shot happiness now far beyond his reach.

So when he woke at sunrise, Idrun's heart was aching for Ligugé. But he jumped off his pallet, ran into the yard towards the well there to wash his face and neck. Here Gunto, a bowl of milk between his hands, found him and whispered:

'Keep away from the hall this morning. Such a bustle going on about the master's dinner, and the mistress, so they tell me, had a bad dream—all about horses without heads—'

Idrun pulled the red smock over his damp shoulders and drank the milk gratefully.

'Has my mother asked for me?'

Gunto shook his head.

'It is a holiday for you today, Idrun.'

'How do you know?'

'The master told my father before going to Troissant.'

Idrun's eyes flashed angrily. 'Grifo should have told me.'

Gunto stretched his hand for the empty bowl and said nothing.

'Didn't you hear what I said?' cried Idrun.

'I am afraid my father forgot,' muttered Gunto, and Idrun's anger vanished like a thin pencil of smoke into the air.

'Don't let us say any more about it,' he said lightly. 'Are you going to work this morning?'

'Hedging.'

'Well, if you want me, I'll be in the shed.' Idrun pointed with his forefinger.

It was cool and shady there; he sprawled on the clay floor, the axe at his feet, and began plaiting moistened rushes for a basket. He had so chosen to spend his holiday because basket-making did not come easily to him, and he did not want to think of his father's return or of Aldis's changed mood.

The sun rose higher and higher. Raising his head for a moment Idrun saw Willa, one of the serving women, come out of the dairy, a large wooden pan of milk held in both hands. A few seconds later, every corner of Clear Water echoed a terrible scream. The men were in the fields; all the women in the house, including Aldis, rushed to the door, and Idrun leapt to his feet, scattering the rushes right and left.

The great gate stood open, and an immense wild boar, his eyes bloodshot, was charging at Willa, the terrible tusks ready to toss her. She screamed again and let go the pan, runnels of frothy milk all over her bare feet, and the milk was no whiter than her face. She did not move.

Aldis, herself rooted in the doorway, saw it all, crippled by a sense of helplessness. She saw Idrun's red smock as he rushed, the

axe held in both hands, and Aldis covered her face. As if from a
distance she heard a roar followed by a sharp whistling noise which
in its turn gave way to a heavy thud, and then Idrun's voice was
raised in triumph.

'So he is alive, he is alive,' murmured Aldis and ventured to
look, her body trembling from her head to her toes.

There lay the monster, Idrun's axe embedded in the head all but
cleft in two. Streams of dark red blood ran all over the grass
colouring the spilt milk and seeping between Willa's toes, as she
tottered forward, knelt before Idrun and kissed his knees. Aldis
wanted to shout, to have her arms round his shoulders, but she had
no strength for either speech or movement, and tottered back into

the house, two of the women attending to her, the rest running off
to fetch Grifo and the other men.

Idrun walked up, and stooping, pulled the axe out of the boar's
head, a great gush of blood splashing all over his feet and legs. The
axe held under the right arm, Idrun stared at the dead monster,
wonder and awe in his grey eyes. Those tusks would have had no
mercy either on him or on Willa. But Idrun felt too bewildered to
take it all in. He had never been taken to a boar hunt but he had
heard so many stories of grown, strong men being tossed and
trampled to death—was it God's mercy or some instinct in him
which had made him aim so true? Idrun could not tell. But he felt
that the morning had turned into a song.

Meanwhile, Grifo and the other men ran into the yard. The
great carcass made them all stand and stare. Then Willa broke out
into an incoherent story where the broken pan, the axe, the spilt
milk, Idrun and a cat were all jumbled together until Grifo shook
the girl's shoulder.

'But who killed the boar?' he shouted. 'What's a cat got to do
with it?'

'She was just behind me,' stammered Willa. 'I tell you—Master
Idrun did it—'

At these words such shouting and clapping broke out in the yard
that Idrun, crimson to the very tips of his ears, ran into the house
to be caught by Malina as soon as he had crossed the threshold.

'Here—' her thick voice spoke
urgently—'the mistress wants
you,' and she pushed Idrun towards the farthest corner of the
hall where Aldis sat, leaning
against the wall. When she saw
him, she raised her arms, the
wide sleeves of her grey gown
falling back, and within an instant Idrun found himself pressed
to her chest.

'My little one, my son,' she

murmured. 'The beast might have killed you—' and she caressed him, stroking his hair, face and neck, kissing his mouth, eyes and forehead, until Idrun leapt away, crouched on the floor, and smiled up at her.

'Well, he did not kill me, Mother. But I must run and scrub myself clean.' He peered at her. 'Oh, dear, you've stained your veil—'

Aldis shrugged it away.

'Go and get clean then. But come back to me.'

Idrun ran, skirting round the house to avoid the men still standing and staring at the dead boar. He reached the little pond at the back, stripped, and plunged right up to his neck. It was glorious to feel the water all over him and the sun over his head. The old thorns edging the pond gleamed palely green, and even the stained red smock and hose flung on the grass added a quality of their own to an incredible morning. He was clean. He felt ravenously hungry. He remembered the whistle he always carried tied to his belt. He jumped out of the water, conscious that the day was a landmark never to be forgotten, and whistled as loudly as he could. Gunto, he felt sure, would find him and fetch him some clean clothes.

Meanwhile, the sun-warmed grass served Idrun's immediate purposes. He rolled over and over again until he was dry, and then sat down, facing the pond, with thorn branches mirrored in the clear dark-blue water.

But Gunto did not come. Hunger began gnawing at Idrun. He picked up the stained smock and got into it. Then, raising his face, he saw his father coming towards him, and he hung his head.

'What a home-coming,' said Berno. 'Did the beast chase you?'

'No, Father, he just ran into the yard and made for Willa—' Idrun stared at his bare toes—'and I—I happened to have my axe by me. That is all.'

'That is all?' Berno echoed thickly. 'A lad of twelve killing a boar—weren't you frightened?'

'I couldn't be, Father. I mean, you taught me how to hold the axe, and fear—well—it does make you shake.' Idrun added, 'I was

terribly scared the moment after—just before he fell . . . I thought
I hadn't killed him—'

Berno put his heavy hand on Idrun's shoulder and his voice rang
unsteady:

'Son, you can ask me anything you like, and it shall be done. I
say so as one Frank to another.'

Here he considered Idrun's clothes and his big mouth smiled
wryly.

'I'll send someone with clean gear for you.'

'Thank you, Father.' Idrun added, 'And thank you too, for your
promise.'

'You'll want some time to think it over, I suppose.'

'Yes, please, Father.'

Berno smiled and turned away, but Idrun did not watch him go.
He did not know what advice Turgot had given but he knew—
and that passionately—that he needed no time to make his
decision. To learn his letters was all he wanted, and could he ask
for his father's consent when the trouble with Ligugé hung, an
angry dark cloud, over him? Idrun clenched his hands tight. He
wanted to cry and he knew he must not. A woman came, carrying
clean clothes in her arms. His back to her, Idrun asked for some
bread and cheese. He wished for no dinner, he said.

The woman mumbled: 'But there is such a meal ready—stuffed
pike and all—'

'Bread and cheese, please,' Idrun repeated.

He was ravenous. But he wished to be alone, to sort out his
thoughts, to make his request, and then . . . He shuddered. Suppose
his father meant to quarrel with the monks. . . . He should have
asked but he had not dared. He sat on the grass, staring at the pond,
and its sunlit loveliness said nothing to him.

It was not a serving woman but Gunto who brought the food to
him. Idrun was glad of the food but he had nothing to say to his
friend.

He wanted most desperately to be alone. The result of his
father's excursion to Troissant did not stir the least curiosity in him.
He needed no time to consider his request; he knew that to a

Frank a promise was binding in honour and that his father could never refuse him now—but in what manner could he, Berno's son and heir, go to Ligugé now?

Never in all his life had Idrun felt so helpless and miserable.

Meanwhile, Berno, having tidied himself, sat on the edge of the bed in the upper chamber telling his wife about Turgot's advice.

'So you are not going to law about it?' she asked tremulously.

'It seems I'd be a fool if I did. And Turgot was so generous, too.' He paused. 'Wife, I think it is time the children were betrothed.'

Aldis bit her lip and said nothing.

'He'll be a man in a year or two,' Berno said slowly, 'now he's proved himself.'

'Proved himself?' she flashed back at him. 'Husband, Idrun is a hero.'

'Don't you put that idea into his mind! I will not have a braggart of a son.'

'Will you reward him?' she asked quickly.

'I told him I'd do anything he asked, and he begged for time.'

'There is only one thing he wants,' Aldis murmured, without looking at her husband, 'and it would be so very awkward.'

Berno said nothing. He got up, pulled back the leather curtain, and shouted to the women below in the hall:

'Fetch Master Idrun, one of you.'

So it happened that the boy was not left alone for long. Head bent, he stood in his parents' room and waited. Berno sighed.

'Well, son, have you thought enough?'

'Yes.'

'And what is it you wish?'

'To learn my letters.' Idrun's cheeks flushed and his breath came jerkily.

Berno bit his lip. 'Listen, son, Master Turgot thinks I'll gain nothing by going to law. So I have decided to drop the matter, and I must keep the promise I gave you, but it might be awkward—' He stopped, Idrun said nothing, and Aldis broke in:

'Priors don't last for ever, husband.'

Berno spread his huge arms.

'Let him go then— I'll send Grifo and a few men with him.'

'After the feast,' Aldis put in firmly, 'in honour—of so many things, husband.' She cast a significant look at Berno.

Idrun was trembling. He could not believe it. 'I am dreaming,' he thought, 'and I'll wake up and there'll be no dead boar, no ride to Ligugé, nothing.' But he knew it was true and his whole world was flooded with light.

'Thank you, Father,' he said shakily, and turned to the stairway.

The killing of a boar meant much work for all the men and women at Clear Water. April nights were still chilly enough, but by daytime the sun shone more and more warmly, and not an hour must be wasted to prepare the carcass. All field labour slipped into the background. None of the serving folk appeared for the noonday meal, Malina having supplied them with bread, a huge milk cheese and jugs of rough cider.

Grifo having organized his forces, some of the men went to a meadow well beyond the kitchen-garden and started digging a huge, deep hole. When finished, its four sides would be lined with moss. Meanwhile the women, their arms laden with faggots and kindling, started making two large fires, a big iron tripdo being stood over one of them. The other fire was fringed all round with thick iron bars.

As soon as the great carcass was dragged in from the yard, Grifo armed himself with a huge long knife and, sweat pouring over his face and neck, began skinning the monster in a most skilful fashion. When he had done, four of the men carried the skin to the fire and stretched it over the iron sticks, two girls from the dairy being told to keep on damping the flames.

'See that the skin is smoked and not singed,' Malina instructed them.

When the carcass was dismembered, Malina came wholly into her own. Not a particle of the boar's flesh was to be wasted, she kept repeating. A huge iron cauldron was hung over the tripod and filled with steaming water, and the offal was thrown into it together with a big crockful of turnips, another of beans, and some salt doled out by Malina herself. The four legs, carefully washed and cleaned, were hung on two sides of the cauldron. The rest of the carcass, cut into many pieces, was cleaned, washed, thoroughly dried, and each piece wrapped in salt-sprinkled linen. When ready those pieces were carried to the moss-lined hole and covered with more moss.

The sun was rising higher and higher. The meadow lay veiled by the thick, acrid smoke from the two fires. The smell of blood, fresh meat, and the savoury fragrance of the stew was everywhere. The women kept drying their hands and necks. The men threw off their smocks, and their white linen breeches were stained with sweat, blood and crushed grass. It was hard work but nobody grumbled. Here and there a hoarse voice broke into a song, and Willa, whilst watching over the skins, had to repeat the great story over and over again, adding piously:

'Death was within a step's distance from me—but Our Lady made the young master rush to my rescue.'

Soon the broth was ready. The heart and the liver were fished out, the long iron spoon deftly handled by Malina. Two other women chopped up the stuff, mixing it with bean flour and eggs, and kneading the mess into fat sausages rather clumsily shaped, but the women licked their fingers appreciatively, and Malina snapped at them:

'Can't you wait for your supper?'

Then she saw her son seated by the moss-lined hole. The grey smock off his shoulders, his hair more matted than usual. Gunto, having carried out a multitude of tasks, wondered if he might slip away and find Idrun.

'What are you sitting idly for?' demanded his mother. 'There is no more cider left. The men are thirsty. Fetch two jugs, and be quick about it.'

She watched him go and looked round triumphantly. They were certainly getting on well with the job and, if kept between stone slabs, the sausages would be all right for the feast. There would be boar's broth for supper, and Clear Water had a young hero of its own. If only a pilgrim or someone would pass their way and carry the great news south, to Poitiers. Such courage, Malina thought, deserved a suitable reward, say a relic to protect Clear Water from thunder and the like calamities. She smiled broadly at them all, and, satisfied that her presence was no longer necessary, made her way across the meadow into the kitchen-garden. There, in the farthest corner, she heard Idrun's excited voice:

'Yes, that is what happened, and you and I are going to ride south as soon as the feast is over—so my father says. Gunto, I am so happy.'

Malina saw the empty jugs at her son's feet, but she slipped back, neither of the boys noticing her. It was something, Malina reflected, to have a hero's friend for a son.

VI

What Happened at Ligugé

It was quite some time before Dom Defensor could see Abbot Ursin. Unluckily for the anxious librarian, one important visitor after another came to the Abbey, and the Abbot could not refuse them even though those frequent abrasions across the day's routine left him exhausted and caused trouble to the infirmarian. Abbot Ursin was old and very frail, and he seldom appeared in choir or shared his meals with the monks. But he was a great scholar, and his fame had winged far beyond the borders of Frankland. In those days of waiting, as Dom Defensor learned, there was the Bishop of Poitiers, the Abbots of St Denis and St Omer, two important scholars from Ireland and Northumbria, all coming to Ligugé to seek advice, confirmation of their own theories about this old manuscript or that, and none of those important visitors could be refused entry to the Abbot's lodgings, and there was nothing for Dom Defensor to do except wait, and the waiting proved a thorny business.

He had finished the preface to his anthology, and was just starting on the Abbey chronicle when Dom Placid appeared to ask if he might borrow a rare manuscript of Augustine's *City of God*. He wished to copy the design of a capital letter, he said. Dom Defensor found the book. The other bowed his head and said awkwardly:

'So the people from Clear Water did not come here this week?'

'No,' Dom Defensor replied curtly.

'I have heard,' Dom Placid went on slowly, 'that Mistress Aldis looked a picture of woe when she left St Cross Abbey. I wonder what gossip the ladies shared with her.'

'I would not know, brother.'

'The men who accompanied her, went to the Golden Grape, and I suppose they must have been instructed not to talk. They just had their meals and they slept. . . .' Dom Placid hesitated. 'Of course, everybody in Poitiers has heard the story.' He paused, the leather-bound book pressed to his chest, his blue eyes very unhappy, and Dom Defensor laid down the quill.

'What story, brother?'

'Well, that we are robbing Clear Water. First a small lake and a little wood—just for a start, see? And now our pious Prior thinks that the whole steading might be of use to Ligugé. Isn't it shameful, Dom Defensor?'

The librarian made no reply. His hands were trembling.

'Please return the book as soon as you have done with it, brother,' he said shakily, but Dom Placid stayed by the doorway.

'Our watchword is "peace",' he said suddenly, sadness creeping into his eyes, 'and what peace is there for a religious house, its prior grabbing right and left!'

'That is for the Abbot to decide,' Dom Defensor said gently.

In less than five minutes he left the cloister, crossed the garth, and reached the stout oaken door of the Abbot's lodging. The pink-cheeked novice opened to his knock and looked ill at ease.

'Father,' he mumbled huskily, 'the lord Abbot has had a poor night. He is very weary today.'

'I am sorry,' murmured the librarian, 'but it is an urgent matter and see him I must.'

The novice stepped back, his face flushed. Within an instant Dom Defensor entered the familiar room, books bound and unbound scattered all over the stone floor, the sloping desk carrying three inkhorns and a mass of parchment sheets. An ivory crucifix of fine Spanish workmanship hung on the wall between two narrow windows and just below was St Bridget's cross, Abbot Ursin's predecessor having come from Ireland. A low stool and a narrow oak table summed up the furniture. The table had a platter on it—with a small piece of pickled fish, some rye bread, an apple and a horn cup of perry. Dom Defensor glanced at it and remembered it was long past the dinner hour.

'He'll probably have it for his supper,' he thought as he knelt by the sloping desk for the old man's blessing.

Abbot Ursin was very old; his face and hands were the colour of ivory and his frailty was accentuated by the black habit, the hood pulled off the finely veined forehead. The sun danced and glanced off the silver cross of office on his breast, and he smiled at Dom Defensor and murmured his blessing.

'I am glad to see you, my son. These last days have been so crowded. I beg you—sit down and tell me of your trouble.' He added, the smile still lighting his face, 'I know you are in trouble. What is it?'

Dom Defensor told the story briefly and simply. The Abbot's thin hand seized a style and he made a few notes on an ivory tablet.

'You were right to come and tell me about it. . . . So the anthology is finished and you have started on the Ligugé chronicle. Well done. God go with you, my son—' and, at the words of dismissal, Dom Defensor got up, bowed and went.

Left to himself, Abbot Ursin stared about as though he expected the walls to fall down. Well, he thought to himself, it was only right that something should happen to him for appointing a scoundrel to be prior. The old man rose slowly to kneel in prayer before the crucifix. Then he returned to the desk and realized that he must strengthen himself for the ordeal facing him. The food tasted like dust, but he ate it dutifully and emptied the horn cup.

The tinkle of a small silver bell brought the pink-faced novice into the room.

'Please, child,' said the Abbot courteously, 'find a brother outside and tell him that I wish to see the Prior.'

'Yes, my lord.'

'But before you go,' the Abbot went on in the same quiet voice, 'you might refill my cup, child. I feel oddly thirsty today.'

The cup was refilled. The Abbot drank it and leafed over some of the many letters he had to answer. It was quite some time before Dom Simeon appeared, his cheeks very red, his eyes staring about, and his hands shaking. According to custom, he knelt for the

Abbot's blessing but did not get it. Nor did the old man invite the Prior to take the stool.

The pink-cheeked novice would hardly have recognized Abbot Ursin: the mild eyes had gone steely, the mouth was drawn into a sharp grim line, and the voice rang harsh:

'I want to hear from you about our dear friends at Clear Water. What has been happening there?'

The Prior's cheeks turned an even deeper red. He gulped twice before replying.

'Nothing has happened, as far as I know, my lord. Master Berno and his son were expected here last week, but they did not come.' He stopped and gulped again, but the Abbot, sitting very straight in his chair, said nothing.

'I suppose—they are very busy—with field work and all—' Dom Simeon broke off, and the old man raised his hand.

'Is that all you can tell me?' There was ice in the Abbot's voice. 'There is much more behind it, isn't there? And you thought that with an old superior, buried in his books, you could do as you pleased. Is it not so?'

Dom Simeon stood silent.

'What authority had you for claiming a lake and a coppice from Clear Water?'

Dom Simeon began breathing a little more easily. If that was all the old man knew, no danger need creep near him, the Prior.

'My lord,' he began persuasively, 'you did me the high honour of appointing me as your chief officer. The interests of this house lie—'

Where was your authority for what you had done?' interrupted the Abbot, and Dom Simeon's consciousness of danger was enlarged.

'There is an ancient charter—'

'I want to see it. Go and fetch it this instant.'

The Prior did not move.

'Do I have to repeat what I have said?'

Dom Simeon bowed and left the room. The old man covered his face with his hands.

'All of it my fault, my own fault—for having trusted the scoundrel,' he murmured under his breath.

In five minutes the Prior, his face no longer red but deathly pale, came back. His hand shook as he laid the tattered piece of parchment on the desk. The Abbot flicked it with a forefinger, looked at it very carefully, read the short piece from end to end, and asked ironically:

'How much did you have to pay for it?'

'Pay for it?' echoed the Prior.

'Yes! Such a very clever fake could not be had for nothing.' Abbot Ursin stroked his beard. 'Dom Simeon, there are just two men in this house who are well acquainted with the Merovingian script, and I am one of them. It is a clever fake, but it is not perfect. This is no more King Clovis's sign manual than my own.' The old man took a knife and very unhurriedly cut the parchment to pieces, Dom Simeon's bulging eyes veiled in terror.

'And are you employing the same rogue of a cleric to prove that the whole steading of Clear Water has really belonged to Ligugé since, say, the day of St Martin? That would be a slightly harder fake to get done.' The Abbot's irony cut like a finely tempered blade. 'Answer my question—who is the rogue?'

Dom Simeon clenched and unclenched his hands. He wished the ground at his feet would open and swallow him up. He moistened his lips.

'I am waiting.' The voice was grim.

'Some time ago, my lord, you sent me to Bourges. The house has property there—a farm or two and some meadowlands—'

'I dislike long prefaces, Dom Simeon,' the Abbot broke in sternly, and the unfortunate Prior fell on his knees.

'It was at one of those farms. The man lodged an old cleric—from Vienne—I think—and we discussed all the difficulties and the old man told me he had an idea. By Our Lady and St Martin, my lord, I had no other motive . . . Clear Water seemed the nearest . . . and—' The web of his incoherency getting more and more tangled, Dom Simeon stopped and bowed his head.

'And I suppose the same old rogue is now working at a scheme to prove that the whole of Clear Water is ours—possibly granted to the monastery by Moses or Jacob,' mocked the Abbot.

Dom Simeon did not answer.

'To fake a charter is an offence at law, and you know it, but I'd rather not drag the miserable business into the open. Stand up, please.'

The Prior straightened himself, but he knew he was shaking. Fear and anger together possessed him. Who could have betrayed him? He did not know, and he was never to know, that the same farmer from near Bourges had been to Poitiers on business, stayed at the Golden Grape and, his natural garrulity greatly swollen by many cups of beer, had boasted that he would have his rent lowered because of Ligugé's branching-out prosperity. Clear Water had been mentioned, and every gossip-monger in the neighbourhood had added a few more stitches of embroidery to the fantastic story. Dom Simeon knew none of that, but his wrath flamed against Berno and even Idrun. 'I'll get even with those two one day,' he thought savagely. 'That stripling hero!'

Meanwhile, the old Abbot leant back in his chair. Sternness had gone from him. He looked very sad.

'I should be doing my duty,' he began very slowly, 'if I sent you to some such prison as St Médard—and that for life. But I can't do it because in a way I share your misdeeds. This house has borne a fair name from the beginning, and you have done your best to defame it. Now, I did not summon a chapter to make you Prior. I exercised my right to choose you because I trusted you, and knew you to be a monk of good judgment and much energy. I am not calling a chapter now. I understand that Dom Tibo has lost one of his underlings. You will take his place as from today.'

Dom Simeon stammered: 'My lord, Dom Tibo is—is a swineherd.'

'Exactly, and you will work under him.' The Abbot made a small gesture of dismissal, watched the other stagger out of the room, and rang the little silver bell again. He felt worn out, but the matter was not finished, and when, at his summons, the fat and jovial Dom Jonas, the secretary, appeared, Abbot Ursin began dictating slowly and clearly:

'I, Ursin, by the grace of God and the free election of my brethren, Abbot of the monastery of Ligugé in the county of Poitou, hereby make known that the Silver Lake and the oak coppice, commonly called The Children's Wood, belong inalienably to Berno of Clear Water and to his lawful successors. Furthermore, I declare and attest that no claim whatsoever against the manor and the lands of Clear Water should ever be lodged by the Abbot and community of Ligugé. In witness thereof I append my hand, duly witnessed by the hand of my scribe, Dom Jonas of the said monastery of Ligugé, and the seal of the Abbey, the said seal entrusted to my keeping by virtue of my office.'

He finished and sighed. Dom Jonas carefully folded his writing tablets and hid them in his pouch. The Abbot spoke very slowly:

My son, see to it that three copies be made of this script. One to remain here, the second to be sent to Paris, and—'

'The third, my lord,' murmured the secretary, whisking the tablets out of the pouch.

Abbot Ursin smiled.

'The third must go to Clear Water, my son.' He paused, head sunk on breast—for he felt very tired. 'I believe not a man there knows his letters, and the sight of a parchment might frighten them. Well, my son, you had best ride to Clear Water and read it out to Master Berno. Please ask him to keep the parchment in safety.'

Dom Jonas hesitated. 'My lord, you have dictated it in Latin—'

'Have the contents put into our tongue,' replied the Abbot, 'and I wish that no discussion of the matter take place in the house.'

'Yes, my lord.'

Abbot Ursin felt so weary that he could not manage to answer any of the several letters on the desk. All the same, he gave some time to prayer, walked a little in his enclosed garden, remarking the fresh beauty of lime leaves, young beech, and fragrant herbs planted here and there. He thought of Clear Water where he had never been and which he was not likely to see, and he thought of the well-mannered grey-eyed boy, one day to be master of the place.

'Didn't Dom Defensor tell me once the boy longed to know his letters?' he thought. 'Well, now that we are friends again, it might be arranged—so long as his father does not object. Didn't Dom Defensor tell me that the hope of the country lay in the young? It always does . . . It always does . . . What is the boy's name? Adrun? No, no, Idrun—'

That evening, for the first time in months, the Abbot supped with his monks in the great vaulted refectory. It was not a feast but an ordinary working-day, and men were astounded to be given fish baked in batter, wheaten bread and perry for their evening meal which usually consisted of a bowl of thin bean porridge and a cup of water. They might not talk since all speech was banned in the refectory except on great festivals but, having looked at their piled-up platters, they exchanged telling glances.

Their amazement deepened when, the long grace chanted, the Abbot took his place at the head of the table. To his right sat an elderly senior monk. To his left was the Prior's place, and Dom Placid, the Abbey's illuminator, occupied it. Farther down the long table, just below Dom Tibo's place, sat Dom Simeon, his face half hidden by the black hood. He applied himself to his food since the Rule demanded it, but the least intelligent among the monks could see that he had no relish for it.

Someone mounted the steps of the lectern and began reading a homily by St Jerome. Nobody heard a word of it. They were enjoying their supper for one thing, and, grace chanted again and the Abbot gone to his lodgings, they all smiled at Dom Placid, the new Prior of Ligugé, and none felt more light-hearted than the librarian.

VII

Full Sunrise for Idrun

Such bustle and hustle were going on at Clear Water that Idrun preferred to spend whole hours, his bow and quiver over his shoulder, in the neighbouring woods, and come back, the game bag full to bursting. His mind was confused; he knew that his mother, delighted at having avoided all legal pitfalls, looked upon the feast as the betrothal day, and that did not interest Idrun at all. He also knew that the grapevine of rumour about his exploits had reached Poitiers, Dame Melita sending a messenger with a present: a relic of St Radegund enclosed in a tiny box of rare Eastern wood, and that angered Idrun.

'There was just nothing in it,' he complained to his father one day when returning home after a morning's hunt, they sprawled on the bank of the stream to wash their dusty feet.

Berno stripped himself to the waist and, plunging both arms into the clear water, began splashing his face and neck.

'A hero! A hero!' Idrun stamped his bare foot on the silken grass. 'I hate the very sound of the word! It's like—like—' he gulped—'everyone pointing their fingers at you. A nice hero indeed, when my knees were shaking with terror.'

'Your arms did not,' Berno said quietly. 'And you are still bent on going to Ligugé?'

'You've given your consent,' the boy muttered, and dipped his toes into the water.

'Well, I don't know what reception you will get there! It might ask for more courage than using your axe. And now tell me—why ever did you begin to wish for it?'

Idrun flushed scarlet. It all seemed so clear to him, and yet he

had no words. He pulled up a blade of grass and chewed it before replying:

'Because I once heard Dom Defensor say that—that even a little learning meant light.'

'So your parents have been in the dark all their lives,' said Berno ironically.

'I did not mean that at all, at all,' cried Idrun, scrambled to his feet and ran homewards.

In the great yard he found Aldis having a serious session with Malina. Some peace-offering must surely be sent to Ligugé when Idrun went there, but what could she send? The monks never ate meat; they kept their own bees and had enough fish. Aldis had no finished embroidery to offer. Here Malina clapped her huge red hands.

'I know, mistress. Monks never hunt, and winters are cold enough. Surely, we could spare two or three coverlets. More,' she added judicially, 'would be a mistake. There are enough wolf and bear pelts and to spare in the store-room, mistress.'

'They are not lined,' sighed Aldis.

'Ah—but I'll set two or three of our girls to get them lined in less time than it takes a spider to weave its web. The young master could not go empty-handed, could he?'

'Have it your way,' Aldis nodded and saw Idrun just about to make for the kitchen-garden. 'Come here, son. What an eel you are these days! There is something you must see.'

Reluctantly enough, Idrun followed his mother into the house. There, in the upper chamber, on a piece of fine linen spread over the coffer, lay a silver buckle and a bangle of fine Greek work, a length of garnet-coloured silk and a gold pin with an oval green stone in its head. Aldis stepped back, triumph in her eyes. Idrun stared at the baubles.

'Who are they for?' he asked at last. 'Your cousin at Poitiers?'

'Oh, you silly! They are your betrothal gifts to Judith.'

'She'll tear the silk to pieces and damage all the rest, Mother.'

'Tear the silk? She'll be allowed to look at them and then I'll keep them safely till the wedding,' said Aldis. 'Look at this gold pin, Idrun, and the bangle. I brought them here as a bride—and now they'll go to your bride.'

Idrun wished he might burst into tears.

'Oh, Mother, you are so generous!'

'All of it is to be yours one day, my son.' She stretched out her right hand and stroked his rough hair. 'But you will remember your manners, won't you, and not hit Judith?'

'So long as she doesn't call me a hero!' he cried. 'Gunto heard his mother talk about the pickled boar's head. I sometimes wish I hadn't got my axe by me that morning. Men go to wars and come back, and nobody calls them heroes.'

She spoke very gently. 'You are not yet a man, Idrun.'

But from her look and the colour of her voice Idrun understood that she approved of his wish not to hear the wild boar story mentioned quite so often.

The day of the feast approached. Grifo and Malina were turned out of their shack because the upper chamber would be occupied by Turgot and Sir Martin. A tall roughly timbered screen was put up to give privacy to Judith and Vorgis. The house breathed with spices all day and all night long. Idrun's feast clothes were ready, and Aldis decided to wear her silver-embroidered veil in her son's honour. In the hall, the great trestle was covered with fine linen, and Malina, her lips pursed, measured the oil for two silver lamps, Berno having decided that nothing should be grudged that day.

'But oil is so scarce nowadays,' ventured Aldis and he silenced her:

'Our son's betrothal is more important than anything else, wife. I would not mind if Malina used the very last drop we have.'

The last day came. All food, drink and bedding were ready. Just before dinner the party from Troissant arrived. Turgot wore new boots, his red tunic was clasped with a huge silver buckle, his hair brushed most carefully, and behind him came Judith, obviously ill at ease in her clean white and red gown and shoes on her feet. Idrun, having grubbed the whole morning in the bean-field, got a frown from Aldis and a cuff from Berno. Before the guests knew he had come in, Idrun found himself dragged away to the well. Washed and spruced up, he returned, bowed to Turgot and kissed Judith's left cheek.

'Ah! Here comes our hero,' she laughed, and clapped her hands. Idrun's cheeks burned red, but he reined in his temper.

'I have some presents for you,' he said gruffly.

They were standing together under one of the old apple-trees in the yard.

'Thank you,' replied Judith so politely that he could hardly believe his ears, and was relieved to see old Sir Martin totter through the gateway.

The noonday meal was of necessity a sketchy affair because of the next day's banquet. Sir Martin was just about to mumble the customary thanksgiving when shouting broke out in the doorway and a wild-eyed, unkempt man, Berno's swineherd, rushed into the hall, hands raised above his head.

'Master, mistress,' he cried, 'they're coming . . . they are nearly at the gate.'

Aldis clenched her hands tightly. Robbers? Surely not in daylight? Tax-collectors to spoil Clear Water's great occasion? As in a mist she saw Idrun beginning to slip towards the doorway and heard her husband's iron voice:

'Stay where you are, son.'

Then he shouted at the swineherd, 'Now, then, Gislo, stop shaking like a reed! Who are coming?'

'The monks, master,' wailed the man. 'Four of them and three men to guard them, and two carts.'

'Holy Mary and St Martin,' breathed Aldis.

She felt sure they were coming to claim the steading. She looked from her husband to the guests. The faces she saw were inscrutable. But Idrun's lips had gone white.

'Well, let's meet them under God's free skies,' said Berno heavily and moved towards the doorway.

He was too late. In less than an instant the plump figure of Dom Jonas, three other monks behind him, loomed at the threshold. Dom Jonas was smiling. His fat hands clutched a big piece of parchment. Aldis did not see the smile. She stared at the parchment, swayed a little, and dropped on her knees.

'I bring you good news, Master Berno,' announced Dom Jonas in a honeyed voice and began reading aloud 'Ego Ursinus . . .'

They all listened reverently. Aldis, still on her knees, not understanding a word of Latin, took the Abbot's message to be a prayer, and kept crossing herself. Sir Martin, vaguely catching the drift of the sonorous sentences, beamed from ear to ear, Berno never took his eyes off Dom Jonas's face, and Idrun, standing close to Judith, forgot all about her and stared at the sky, his mouth wide open and his eyes starry. The serving folk followed their mistress's cue and continued crossing themselves with the exception of Malina whose mind was engrossed by extra provision of food, drink and bedding for four wholly unexpected guests.

'The fat one,' she thought, 'had best go to the upper chamber, and oh! these holy ones never touch meat, do they?'

Meanwhile, having finished with the Latin text, Dom Jonas translated it into the vulgar tongue, and he had to stop at every sentence, so wild were the cheers, so loud the clapping. He finished at last and mopped his forehead. Before Berno or Aldis found their voices, Malina, her great arms akimbo, forged her way well ahead and asked loudly:

'Are you allowed to eat meat? Such ham we've got and other things—' she licked her thick lips—'but I doubt if there would be enough fish to go round. It is a feast we are holding tomorrow, see?'

'Malina,' cried Aldis, 'how dare you!'

She looked angry and so did Berno, but Dom Jonas, having winked at his brethren, guffawed, and the tension vanished.

'We are travellers,' he said in a voice of mock gravity, 'we eat whatever the good God sends us on our journeys—' He bowed to Aldis, and Malina stumped back into the house.

The serving folk left the yard. Berno and Aldis stood close together, and the former muttered:

'So your Prior has not had his own way, has he?'

'Our Prior,' Dom Jonas replied, 'is now Dom Placid.'

A small silence fell. Quite obviously, the Abbot's secretary did not mean to mention Dom Simeon's name, let alone plunge into the story of his downfall, and courtesy forbade the master of Clear Water to ask prying questions.

'You are all welcome to the feast,' he said simply, and the four monks bowed, when Dom Jonas's glance fell on Idrun.

'Ah! this is your son.' His small eyes considered Idrun. He came forward and laid his fat hand on the boy's shoulder. 'Our librarian is expecting you.'

Later, Idrun could not clearly remember either the feast or his betrothal. Both seemed as remote as though they did not concern him in the least. He walked about in a golden haze, carried out his customary daily jobs, but even when fetching water from the well or gathering kindling for Malina, his mind was absorbed in one idea: that he was going to Ligugé to learn reading and writing. Such a radiant look was in his eyes that even Judith did not tease him. He ate and drank whatever was put before him, but the good food was nothing to him.

At dawn, on the day of the feast, he woke and ran out to scan the skies. Pale blue they were, lightly brushed with grey here and there, but Idrun, sniffing the air, knew that the fine weather was unlikely to break. Bare-legged, a torn smock over him, he ran all over the familiar corners of Clear Water, at once glad of the day's holiday and impatient to see it end, and by an old thorn at the edge of the kitchen-garden he came on Judith.

Vorgis had done her best; she had combed Judith's ravelled hair and secured it with a crimson snood. In a white gown buckled at the left shoulder and girdled with a sash of fine red silk, her little scarlet shoes just peeping from under the folds of the gown, Judith looked something of a stranger but the wildness remained. She stared at Idrun and stamped her foot.

'I am not going to be betrothed to a vagrant,' she cried. 'Your smock! Your feet! And how many years ago did you have your hair combed?'

Idrun clenched his fists. It was an effort to remember the promise given to his mother, but he kept it.

However, that proved the only abrasion, and a very slight one, during the day. Quickly enough the women made Idrun presentable. His scarlet shoes and plaited leggings gleamed in the sun. The new tunic, so carefully stitched by Aldis, sported a heavy buckle of chased silver given by Berno. Idrun held himself up, head and shoulders erect, as he came into the hall and took his place by Judith's side.

The betrothal would have been over soon enough were it not for a wordy argument between Sir Martin and Dom Jonas. The former mumbled that it was fitting for the Abbot's secretary to officiate. The monk protested that it was the duty of Idrun's parish priest. Sir Martin's replies were confused and mostly irrelevant. Dom Jonas's words were winged with subtle theology. Aldis understood nothing. Berno and Turgot frowned. Dom Jonas ended the matter by walking off into the farthest corner of the hall. Sir Martin sighed, pulled at his shabby but clean cassock, muttered a brief prayer, joined the children's hands, and gave his blessing. Gifts were exchanged. Idrun kissed Judith's left cheek and she, standing on tiptoe, kissed his right cheek. Berno and Turgot, neither being literate, put each his cross at the foot of a small piece of parchment, its contents explained by Dom Jonas. Judith's dowry was rich enough: in addition to clothes, bedding and jewellery, she would bring—on her father's death—all the Troissant lands. Berno looked pleased. Idrun's eyes were downcast. Troissant had never meant much to him, his heart being given to Clear Water.

The ceremony over, the guests began thinking of their dinner. Under the warm May sunshine, they wandered about the courtyard, talking in a desultory fashion about the world's affairs. Idrun sought out Gunto and vanished with him somewhere behind the house. Judith was left alone to contemplate the splendour of her betrothal gifts.

Aldis plunged into last-minute activities when Malina, in between breaking the eggs for the batter, told her that Idrun had gone wandering— 'All in his best clothes, mistress.'

Aldis shrugged impatiently. 'Ah—but he has promised not to tumble into mischief.'

There were the presents for Ligugé. To the four neatly lined fur coverlets was added a large piece of heavy cream-coloured silk of Spanish weaving. Aldis had meant to give it to Judith on the wedding-day fixed for All Saints' tide two years hence. 'But what will the child do with it?' Aldis thought and frowned as she remembered that on Midsummer's Day Judith would come and stay at Clear Water and learn housewifely duties.

'I mustn't hurt her father's feelings,' thought Aldis, 'but I will not have this stupid Vorgis come here. Why, Judith is the same age as Idrun and has never held a needle in her life! I'll wear

myself to the bone trying to train and tame her.' She threw down
a piece of linen meant as a wrapping for the Spanish silk, and her
fine grey eyes clouded. 'I wish that wild boar had never crashed
his way here! To let Idrun go to Ligugé—'

The thought reminded Idrun's mother of yet another job: the
lad's clothes, packed in undressed pelts, lay in a corner of the land-
ing. On top of the bundle was a much smaller one wrapped in a
square of dark blue silk. It contained two large silver spoons with
horn handles, a new knife sheathed in Spanish leather, Idrun's
horn cup rimmed with silver, and a small bag of silver coins to
which Berno had added two heavy gold bezants. The contents of
the bag were to assure Idrun's bed and board at Ligugé for nearly
two years. Aldis unpacked the big bundle and went over each
article with quick, trembling fingers. No, nothing had been
forgotten. She rose, wiped the tears off her cheeks, and remembered
that she was mistress of Clear Water and hostess to her guests.

Meanwhile, Idrun and Gunto sprawled on a mossy bank
beyond the kitchen-garden, Gunto having thoughtfully provided
a horse-cloth to spread on the ground for his friend.

'Two years!' he said for the fourth time. 'Why, Idrun, I'll be a
grown man when you come back.'

'I'll be here for a bit later in the summer,' murmured Idrun, 'and
next Easter, too—'

'And you'll find Judith spinning and weaving and stitching all
day long,' said Gunto, and Idrun sighed.

'I'd rather she remained as she is—'

'What? A spitfire, always ready to scratch and bite?'

'Well, am I an angel?' retorted Idrun as he plucked several
blades of grass and started plaiting them.

'I say,' Gunto began diffidently, 'you are so much at home
here—birds, dogs, cattle, plants and trees and all of it. Isn't it
enough? Look at our master. Look at Judith's father. They are
content.'

'But I am not,' Idrun said calmly. 'You see, Gunto, life seems so
much more.... Whenever I've been to that little library at Ligugé,
I'd feel—' he frowned, searching for a comparison— 'why, like

a bird flying free under the skies, or a fish swimming. ...' Idrun
paused, his eyes alight. 'No, not a fish ... but a bird—I can't put
it any better—'

Here, the clang of an iron bell reached them and they leapt up
and reached for the house.

But, later, Idrun could not remember the feast and the long,
long hours that followed. Judith had hoped to see him take his
share in the games, but even the traditional bow and arrows
contest did not attract him. Already, in his mind, Idrun was
journeying southwards, nearer and nearer to his friend. At
break of dawn Aldis's tears and caresses
certainly moved him, but his urgency
to start was so obvious that his mother
loosened her arms and let him mount
one of Berno's horses. Idrun bent down
and smiled, and the smile lit up his whole
face as the little party with Grifo at the
head and four of Berno's men at the rear
moved out of the gateway.

A slight drizzle had been falling all
through the night, the track was coated
with slippery mud, and the horses felt
their way carefully. They were nearing
the first bend when a shout from the
back made all the men turn their heads.
Idrun saw and blushed deep crimson.

It was Judith, her hair all wild, her
gown spattered with mud, her bare feet
stumbling and slithering. She panted as
she ran, her right hand clutching a small
package wrapped in grey linen.

'I did say good-bye to her,' thought
Idrun angrily, but in less than an instant
he reined in. Bare-legged and dishevelled, Judith seemed far more attractive
than when wearing important clothes.

'I've forgotten, I've forgotten,' she cried, drew a difficult breath, flung the little package into Idrun's hands, and turned back, running, regardless of the mud under her feet.

The monks' faces were impassive. Grifo and the other men exchanged glances. Grifo muttered to one of them:

'She is sure to get a hard beating from the mistress! Running about as though she were a serf's child.'

Idrun did not hear it. He had slipped the package into his pouch. Not until they had reached the Golden Grape at Poitiers and he felt assured of comparative privacy, did he unwrap Judith's parting gift.

It pleased him. It contained nothing but six square sheets of virgin parchment.

VIII

Idrun at Ligugé

'I shan't sleep tonight,' thought Idrun as he stood watching his man prepare his bedding in a corner of the common upper room at the Golden Grape. Poitiers seemed so noisy and airless and dirty. Dom Jonas and the other monks had gone to St Martin's Hospice, but there was no room for Idrun, and he must stay at the inn. Grafo, the keeper, had done his best for the son of an important customer: a roughly timbered screen had been set up in Idrun's corner and the floor seemed clean enough. His supper had been brought upstairs—a bowl of savoury stew, some fish baked in batter and a piece of honeycake. There was even a ewer full of water for washing and a linen napkin. The men from Clear Water would sleep just outside the screen, but all the preparations and comforts irked rather than pleased Idrun. The food eaten, he slipped out of his clothes—the room was so hot and airless—and crouched low on the pallet.

Smells, smoke, shouts, laughter and singing came from the room below. Grafo's door was kept open day and night; travellers, pilgrims, merchants, anyone with a coin or two in his pouch got a welcome, and the more they spent, the better Grafo was pleased, his glossy fat cheeks covered with sweat. Berno, as Idrun knew, called the man a swindler and a scoundrel, but Berno was wrong: Grafo gave good value for money. He and his three men could not always prevent an angry argument breaking into a fight, but no murder had ever happened at the Golden Grape—unlike so many Frankish hostelries at the time, when the innkeeper himself was not above cutting a guest's throat.

They talked of omens and prodigies, of the Pope's quarrels with the Lombards, and Duke Charles's reluctance to come to the

Pope's help. They talked of the terrible Saracens and the growing piracy up and down the Mediterranean where no Christian ship was really safe from the marauders. They talked of the appalling state of Frankish roads, the impoverishment on the land, the poor harvests and so many empty market stalls. And, as Idrun listened, he could not help wondering why all those people who kept grumbling, cursing and bewailing their lot, had so much money to spend since, in between, they kept shouting their orders for more food and more drink. Occasionally, the sharp chink of a dropped coin reached Idrun in his screened-off corner.

But soon enough he stopped listening. He had so hoped to reach Ligugé that evening—but the ride through Mal Forest had proved too much for Dom Jonas. He had parted with Idrun in the doorway of the Golden Grape, telling him not to linger over his breakfast in the morning.

'We leave at daybreak, son,' he had said, and Idrun had hidden his disappointment as best he could.

'I'll keep awake all night,' he said to himself, but even the several noises from the room below could not make him keep that vigil: excited, tired, and still angry at the unexpected delay, Idrun fell fast asleep.

The next morning bore hard on Idrun; the day broke, gilding the roofs and spires of Poitiers, but neither Dom Jonas nor any other monks appeared at the Golden Grape. Leaving his father's men to settle with Grafo, Idrun ran fast to St Martin's Hospice. A pilgrim or two just about to leave looked at him with astonishment: Idrun had forgotten to brush his hair and to buckle his red tunic which had slipped off the shoulder.

The doorkeeper was gruff.

'Dom Jonas?' he echoed. 'Why, he and another are gone to the market, and I heard there is a message to be left at St Cross. What may you want with him?'

'Want with him?' cried Idrun, his mouth trembling. 'Why, he is taking me to Ligugé. He said he would be at the Golden Grape to fetch me—at daybreak.'

The doorkeeper shrugged. He was a tall, portly man with a reddish beard and small green eyes, and something about him reminded Idrun of Dom Simeon.

'I know nothing about it,' the man said in a surly voice. 'To provide bedding for pilgrims and to keep order is my business, not Dom Jonas's affairs.' His hostile eyes peered at Idrun. 'Anyway, no monk from Ligugé may enter an inn, didn't you know that? And if I were you, lad, I'd make myself tidy.'

'When will Dom Jonas be back?'

'He did not tell me,' and the man closed the door in Idrun's face.

Never had he felt so miserable and so abandoned. He stood still for a few moments, then fumbled in his pouch, found his buckle and pinned it to the tunic. His left hand smoothing his ravelled hair, he came to a decision.

'I'll go back to the Golden Grape and tell Grifo to have the horses saddled, and we'll ride to Ligugé! A message to be left at St Cross! The ladies will probably urge him to stay to dinner.'

There was, however, no need for Idrun to give any orders: the horses were ready at the door and all the gear brought from Clear Water packed into saddle-bags. When the men heard Idrun's story, one of them laughed.

'Eh—young master—that's the way with all those holy folk. Can't tell today from yesterday!' He threw back his head and scanned the sky. 'It is sure to rain after noon,' he whistled, 'and Dom Jonas doesn't like getting wet.'

'We are leaving now,' said Idrun imperiously and leapt on the back of his shaggy pony.

Just at that moment he saw Jonas and the others rounding a corner, and he blushed deep red as he leapt down.

'I—I—thought you'd forgotten,' he muttered.

Dom Jonas laughed. 'I had forgotten to tell you. Dom Placid asked me to get him a few pots of paint—I should have told you—' he hurried on, 'but I did not remember until we got to the hospice.'

'I—I went there—'

'Did you? Well, the doorkeeper knew all about it.'

Idrun, still blushing, said nothing, and all of them moved south-wards and, with the town well behind them, Idrun began breath-ing freely. The wind roughened a bit but the sun still shone, and the road to the Abbey, curving here and there, led them through an enchanted, fragrant green world until the gilded spire and towers of the basilica made Idrun forget everything in the world except that he was on his way to learn his letters.

He had been to the Abbey often enough. It used to be so simple: his duty paid to the Abbot, Idrun would make his way to the west cloister and the library, and there enjoy himself, some-times listening to Dom Defensor, sometimes watching him at work. Of course, those sessions would be broken off by the ring of a bell summoning the monks to an office or a meal, but some-how Idrun was so used to those silvery bells that they were no longer so many tiresome interruptions: rather they came to enlarge all he learned from his friend.

But this time everything was different. Once past the gateway, Dom Jonas told the porter's assistant to fetch the guest-master, and Idrun had no choice but to wait and watch his father's men unpack the bulging saddle-bags. He noticed that the bundle containing his personal belongings was put aside.

Several minutes passed but the guest-master did not appear. At last, Dom Jonas nodded to Idrun and made towards the great garth—obviously on his way to the Abbot's lodging. Idrun moved to follow him but the porter checked him.

'Dom Alexis is on the way here,' he said quietly.

Idrun bit his lips. He was burning with impatience to get to the west cloister. He did not know that, since Ligugé had no school, quite special arrangements had to be made for him, Berno's son, that he had not come on a few hours' visit but for several months and that, finally, very few things were explained to curious laymen coming to Ligugé and none at all to boys of his age.

So Idrun waited, his cheeks as red as his tunic and his hands trembling a little. Was Dom Defensor ill? Would he, Idrun, have to ride back to the Golden Grape, spend another night in that smoky, noisy place, and then take the road to Clear Water, his ambition and desire turned to shrivelled beech leaves? He was a Frank, and he had known for years that Frankish men and boys did not cry, but he remembered a pilgrim from Rome coming to Clear Water.

'There, even grown men weep like women,' he had said contemptuously, and now, waiting for the guest-master, Idrun wished himself beyond the Alps, at liberty to shed as many tears as he pleased.

'Here he is,' muttered one of the men behind him, and Idrun saw a very tall, lean monk coming towards them. The red beard, the clear blue eyes, and the smile, everything about Dom Alexis cheered and heartened people. He had the air and the manner of a man who could be pleasant host to a brigand, and his voice certainly reconciled Idrun to the tiresome abrasions of the morning.

'Welcome, my son. Come with me,' and he beckoned to one of the men to follow them.

Idrun dared greatly and asked:

'Please, sir, is Dom Defensor well?'

The guest-master laughed.

'Indeed yes, and waiting for you too. I believe there is something he wants you to see. But I must take you to your lodging first—such is our rule.'

They had not far to go. They passed a row of workshops, a great bakery, turned a corner, crossed a small unpaved yard, and there was the guest-house, a grey-pink one-storied building, its several unglazed windows enhancing its air of hospitality.

Dom Alexis was saying:

'I have put you in a corner nearest a window. Come winter you shall have a candle—all the windows are shuttered then. You will do your studies in the library—but here you will sleep and eat.'

He bent his head at the entrance, and Idrun followed him.

The guest-house was just one long fairly wide room, all the windows facing south. Quite a number of pallets were arranged along the walls. In the middle stood a long oak trestle surrounded by several wooden stools. A great earthenware jug stood at one end of the trestle, and a crude iron crucifix hung on the wall facing the entrance. There seemed no other furniture. The place was cool and clean. As Idrun stood, observing his new surroundings, Dom Alexis gestured towards a corner.

'Those were the lord Abbot's instructions,' he said. 'You see, son, sometimes Dom Defensor has visitors from other libraries, and the Abbot thought it would be better if you could work here.' He added pleasantly, 'We have no guests at all in the winter.'

Idrun gasped when he saw 'the corner' appointed to him. There hung a leather curtain now drawn back; there lay a pallet with a coffer at its foot. Just under the window stood a small sloping desk with a square stool in front of it. A tall dark-yellow candle in an iron stick neighboured an inkhorn and a bunch of styles. All in all, it was a miniature study, and Idrun had never expected any such carefully detailed arrangements made for his comfort. He blushed for pleasure and for shame, too, as he remembered his wildly impatient mood earlier in the day.

'I know,' the guest-master was saying, 'that you will keep it all tidy. There is a besom, you see. We have no servants here. Dinner and supper are brought by two brothers from the kitchens, but you wash your platter and cup in that stone trough in the yard. We expect our guests to attend the early Mass, to wash their hands before they eat, and to be here when they hear the Compline bell.' He smiled and laid his hand on Idrun's shoulder. 'There are no other rules—you are free to wander all over our meadowlands when Dom Defensor is busy. And now you can't see the lord Abbot—he is none too well—so you had better make for the library. Know the way, do you?'

Idrun nodded. There was something he knew he must say, but he had a feeling as though all words were rabbits scurrying here, there and everywhere. He swallowed his breath and stammered:

'Sir—I—I—never—I mean . . .' His grey eyes starry, he gestured at the little paradise in the corner.

'I understand, son,' Dom Alexis said quietly. 'God go with you.'

The sun had vanished behind a fleeting cloud shaped like a lyre, but the whole world was golden when Idrun reached the west

cloister. Dom Defensor, the shabby black hood pulled over his forehead, greeted him as simply as though they had met the day before.

'Welcome, son.' The old man got up from his stool and moved towards one of the shelves. 'You come in time. See, I have finished

my book.' And Idrun, fascinated, stared at the shelf. All the sheets
of parchment were neatly sewn together and bound between two
stout wooden boards, Dom Defensor's signature being carved on
one of them.

'I did not do the binding,' the old man said. 'I am no good at
carving, son. Dom Placid, I should say the Prior, set one of his
brothers to do it.'

'But it is your book,' breathed Idrun. 'I have seen you work at
it so often and you would never tell me what it was about. You
said I must wait till it was finished'—his smile was disarming—
'and I have waited.'

'The book is not mine,' Dom Defensor said calmly. 'I would
borrow books from St Omer, St Denys and other abbeys and,
as I read them, I would often come on a sentence that struck a
light, and then I would copy it word for word.' He stopped, and
sighed. 'It has taken me a very long time, son, but it is done now.
You see, with the infidels passing all over Spain, who knows
what troubles may fall upon us? Why, whole libraries may be
burned to cinders in Frankland, but I mean to take great care of
my little book. . . .' He paused for a moment. 'Idrun, it is the
cream of many men's thoughts, you see. So I have called it the
book of lights. The prologue alone is my own. Would you like
me to read it to you? You have no Latin—but I'll try and put it
tidily into our tongue.'

Idrun listened. The old man's voice rose and fell in carefully
modulated cadences. It was prose that he read, but to Idrun it
sounded like poetry.

'Reader, whoever you may be, I beg you to read my little book
with understanding. From the words of the Lord and those who
loved Him truly has this spark been struck. I have read many
books with great attention, and sometimes I would come on so
brilliant a sentence that I knew I must put it into my book. Thus
the fire of many great thoughts is gathered together in one little
volume. Even as a harbour is welcome to a mariner, so has this
work been to me. Hear what Augustine said to my heart: "A
just man is afraid of nothing because nothing can make him

afraid," and Pope Gregory is so reassuring: "Instead of running after your enemy with a sword, pursue him with a prayer."'

Idrun crouched on the floor, his lips half-opened, and his eyes full of light.

'I wish,' he stammered, 'I wish I knew Latin.'

'You are to learn it.' Dom Defensor smiled, and put the book back on the shelf.

Idrun clenched his hands so hard that his knuckles went white.

'I wonder what made you do that book,' he stammered, 'with just a preface of your very own—'

'Because these are most uncertain times, son, and it may well be that some great libraries will perish. So I have gathered these little stars together in case.' Dom Defensor shrugged his bony shoulders.

'Is it the Saracens? My mother blames them for everything. If a cow drops her calf, or the porridge is burnt, or my father has stomach trouble, it is always the fault of the Saracens.' Idrun hurried on: 'I once asked her who they were, and she could not tell me except that she had heard that they were not Christian and had a god of their own called Mohammed.'

'They are not Christian,' said Dom Defensor, 'but Mohammed is not their god but their prophet. They are a cruel people and fearless.'

Here a tinny bell broke on them from a distance.

'That is the dinner,' said the monk. 'You'll find the way to the guest-house, son? And be back after Nones for your first lesson.'

The great cool room was empty when Idrun reached it. At one end of the long trestle his knife, platter and mug were set out. Excited as he was, he remembered he had not washed his hands. Dipping them into the cool water of the stone trough, he kept repeating to himself, 'I am here . . . I am starting to learn this very day . . . I am here—at Ligugé.'

A fat little barrel of a monk, his cheeks red and glossy from the heat of the kitchen, appeared round a corner.

'Come along, lad,' he cried and raised a well-laden trencher above his head. 'It is a pigeon pie for you today and an apple.

Dom Alexis said you were not to have beer, but I have brought you some cranberry water.' He shuffled past Idrun, set the food on the trestle, and licked his lips. 'You are not to leave a crumb, see, and when you have washed the crocks, put them outside the door. Ah,' he shook his head, 'learning comes hard on an empty stomach. When I was a novice—long before you were born, lad— we'd sweat at our books, and sweat in the fields, too, and all we got was fish and porridge, porridge and fish, with some honey-bread on feast days. But you are not here to become a monk, are you?'

'No, sir.'

'Well then, cross yourself and eat your fill. And my name is Dom Paul, lad. As I was saying, that hungry we were . . .' he sighed, 'what with fasting and all, and one day the lord Abbot had the Count to dinner, and I had to serve it. Well, there was a large hunk of wheaten bread left and a lot of meat on a pork bone, so I feasted in secret—'

'But—'

'We are not saints here,' interrupted the monk. 'We hope to get to Paradise one day, but that is far harder than learning your letters.' He chuckled and waddled away.

Alone, Idrun stared at the food. A pigeon pie was a luxury, but he felt too excited to eat. 'Not a crumb to be left,' Dom Paul had said and, having crossed himself, Idrun sat down on a stool and took his knife out of its leather sheath.

'My first lesson—after Nones,' he thought, hunger gaining over excitement.

The days shaped themselves into an orderly pattern. Rarely enough, a pilgrim or two appeared in the guest-house, but such as came spent their time in devotional exercises, kept silent at meals and, Compline over, sought their pallets. Dom Alexis and the fat monk from the kitchens paid their daily visits. Idrun, taken to the Abbot's lodging, presented his parents' offering, answered a few questions, and was dismissed with a smile and a blessing. Early enough he learned not to speak to any monk except when they spoke to him; to greet what visitors he met with a bow; to obey the summons of many bells. Within a fortnight, he knew himself at home, waking at dawn to con over the day's lessons, spending the morning with Dom Defensor, learning not only grammar but various other things—the slow and rather smelly preparation of ink, the tedious process of getting a rough sheet of parchment smooth enough for the pen. As each day went, Idrun felt that more and more windows were being opened in his life. As a teacher, Dom Defensor was without a peer at Ligugé: clear, patient and very firm, sometimes severe.

The dinner eaten, Idrun would wander far beyond the Abbey walls, over the meadows, bean fields, woods, along the steep curving banks of the Clain. Here and there, he would come on monks at their work, their habits tucked up above their knees. They dug, fished, hedged and trenched—the Abbey possessions demanded much labour, and all of it was given willingly, un-hurriedly, in the manner of men dedicated to their work. One hot July afternoon, Idrun plunged into a ride across a great oak wood, with pigs rootling under the silvery-green boles of the trees; he saw a monk he had not met before and, standing close by, in a shabby stained habit, with a swineherd's curved staff in his left hand, was Dom Simeon. The older monk bowed to Idrun. Dom Simeon turned away, an angry flush over his face.

'So that is what happened to him—all for the harm he tried to bring to my father's door,' thought Idrun and turned back, resolved to answer anger by anger, but Dom Simeon had moved away from the broad ride, and Idrun did not follow him.

It was the same evening that Idrun heard about his mother and Judith staying at St Cross in Poitiers.

'You shall have a holiday tomorrow,' Dom Defensor told him. 'You are to leave immediately after Mass and get back here when you have had your dinner at our hospice.' He added, 'We'd much rather you did not go to the Golden Grape—hardly a place for a boy on his own.'

Idrun said nothing.

'You will surely be glad to see them?'

'Oh yes—' but the boy's voice sounded uncertain, 'but that would mean missing my lesson—and I'll be going to Clear Water next month.'

Dom Defensor broke in:

'But she is your mother, Idrun, and you are betrothed to the girl.'

'I am,' Idrun said uncomfortably. 'She gave me those sheets of parchment . . .' Suddenly he burst out: 'But it is my lessons. . . . Sir, I've thought of nothing else since I came to Ligugé.'

The weather broke in the night, and Dom Paul and Idrun rode to Poitiers under a canopy of soft grey rain. The monk made for the hospice and told Idrun how to come to St Cross on foot.

'Don't be late for dinner,' he warned the boy.

Idrun came to St Cross's wicket too early, the portress telling him that Mistress Aldis was still at her prayers. He was shown into a bleak narrow slit of a room and Judith came in. He hardly knew her—so trim and tidy she looked in a fresh green gown, her hair brushed, and her bare feet clean.

Idrun bowed awkwardly and kissed her left cheek. He did not quite know what to say, but Judith was at no loss for words.

'You have changed! You are not going to be a monk though because we are betrothed. Oh, Idrun, I wish I were at Troissant! Vorgis would be rough at times, but she is a servant. She could not make me do what she wanted.'

'Aren't they kind to you at Clear Water?' Idrun asked stiffly and added, 'Thank you for the parchment. When I get home in August I mean to find you a present.'

Judith interrupted:

'Kind? Well, I suppose it is time I learned something—but it is hard, Idrun. The other day your mother set me to make three milk cheeses. . . . It was such a lovely day—for running about in the wood, or just idling by the Silver Lake, and the dairy smelt so sour—and I found a dead mouse outside and slipped it into the the milk set for supper, and that dreadful fat Malina caught me at it and complained to Mistress Aldis and she ordered me to be beaten hard. I did not mind the beating—' here Judith's nostrils flew up in scorn—'but is it fitting that a freed serf's wife should beat a free-born Frankish girl? Malina did—'

'Still—' Idrun shuffled his feet on the cold stone floor, 'to put a dead mouse in the milk was stupid.'

Judith put out her tongue at him.

'You would say so! And the very day after I got one of the mares out and had the ride of my life.'

'Well?' There was not much encouragement in Idrun's voice.

'Your mother said I was to fast the whole day, stay indoors, and hem napkins—' Judith bit her underlip. 'Once we are married, Idrun, I'll never, never hold a needle in my hand. I'll make the women do the work. Such a nasty, sharp thing a needle is, and whenever I happen to break one, your mother slaps me.'

'And I'll slap you if you go talking like that about her,' shouted Idrun.

'Why don't you try then?' Judith mocked him.

Within an instant they were at it and felt perfectly happy, giving each other punch for punch and blow for blow until Judith's carefully combed hair became a tangle, her cheeks a wild red, and the right sleeve of her new gown hung in tatters. They stopped to draw a much needed breath. Idrun, himself sorrily dishevelled, a big rent in his tunic, and his nose bleeding a little, stepped back and laughed.

'You are not changed a bit for all the slapping you have had at Clear Water.'

'Nor are you,' she panted, 'for all your Latin learning.'

'How is Gunto,' he broke in impatiently, 'and have you seen many herons on the Silver Lake, and has Gilla foaled?'

But he was never to hear about Gunto or the herons, or his favourite mare. Voices were heard in the distance, and Judith slipped away from the cold, unfriendly room, and Idrun hurriedly smoothed down his hair. His nose had stopped bleeding, but he felt blood drying on his chin and the torn tunic could not be disguised. Still panting, he rubbed at his chin and within a minute a leather curtain was drawn aside. Aldis and Dame Melita stood and stared. The former gasped and cried:

'Idrun, did you have a fight with anyone in the street? Look at your tunic! And there is blood all over your face.'

'I did not fight anyone, Mother,' he replied sulkily, and Dame Melita's mannered little speech enraged him.

'Perhaps he met with another wild boar on the road from Ligugé, cousin. Still, they might have tidied him up at St Martin's Hospice! Never mind, cousin,' she went on fussily, 'I'll send a sister with a basin of warm water, a comb and a needle. It is fortunate that we have some scarlet thread in the house. We will have him neat in no time,' and Dame Melita floated out of the room.

Aldis sighed and sat on a stool. Her green gown and silver embroidered veil gained in beauty against the dull grey stone wall.

'She is lovelier than ever,' thought Idrun and heard her say sharply:

'You did not fight anyone in the street. So it must have been Judith.' Aldis's lips drew into a thin line. 'And I had her put on her new gown because of your visit—'

'Please, Mother, I started it.'

'You? Why?'

He did not answer.

'Why?' she repeated, and Idrun met her look with one of his own.

'I could never tell you,' he replied clearly. 'A Frank's word is his bond—so Father says.'

Aldis opened her lips, when two nuns appeared, their arms laden with a basin of steaming water, a couple of napkins, a comb, a big bobbin of thick scarlet thread and a long bone needle. Idrun, all within him an angry tumult, had to submit to their ministrations. By the time they had done and vanished, Aldis had forgotten her son's obstinacy, and launched into a quick, breathless monologue where her concern for his life at Ligugé was intermingled with complaints about Judith until Idrun could hardly tell where one began and the other ended which was just as well: his mother expected no replies.

'Are you warm enough at night? Do they work you very hard? Really, I am in despair about Judith. She is only happy when she roams about the countryside. Just suppose a bear or a wolf got her! Do you ever get meat for dinner? They don't make you fast, do they—not too often, I mean. I do my best to train her, Idrun, but it is such hard work. Do you get any seasoning with your food? The other day I set the girl to patch one of your father's smocks, and she left the needle in! And can anyone teach her to cook? Do they wash your shirts and drawers, or do you have to do it yourself? I am sure your father feels Troissant will cost us dear. And ah the waste, my son! The other day I told Judith to boil a leg of pork, and she set on and forgot all about it, and the meat was just like straw! Do they allow you to gather wild berries? Yes, I always blame that fool Vorgis. She should have trained Judith! Are you really comfortable at the guest-house? What is the good of a daughter-in-law who likes nothing better than to run wild and to laugh after a beating.'

'I am glad she does laugh. Please, Mother, don't be too hard on her'—and Idrun added, surprising himself: 'I think I like her just as she is.'

Aldis stared.

'What! And a mouse in the milk! And I am sure it was Judith who had put a dead toad in Malina's bed.'

'I'd have put ten,' Idrun broke in.

His mother shrugged and stooped to untie a bundle at her feet. It contained presents she had brought: jars of wild berry preserves, a dressed wolf-skin for a coverlet, a red belt, a small bag of spices and another of salt. Idrun thanked her, but he felt that the morning was going on leaden feet. He had so hoped to hear about Clear Water, the golden oaks in the wood behind the house, all the movement and the music of the place. But there had been nothing of that.

Dame Melita came again, appraised Idrun's tidy appearance, and smiled at him. He kissed Aldis, bowed to the nun, and made his way to St Martin's Hospice where a crowd of weary, shabby and distinctly smelly pilgrims sat on the rush covered floor and waited for their dinner.

Dom Paul, standing by the doorway, led Idrun to a shadowy corner there to struggle with some tepid bean flour porridge and a piece of boiled fish laid on a stale slice of barley bread. A none too clean iron spoon was provided for the porridge but there was no knife and Idrun had to eat the fish with his fingers. Then he slipped past the rows of pilgrims busily discussing their food, grumbling at the quantity doled out, and exchanging stories of visions, miracles and portents. Idrun heard:

'It was to the north of St Médard, friends, that I saw that cloud—with horns at one end and cloven hoofs at the other—and it stayed motionless for the space of one Paternoster—'

The others hurriedly put down their spoons and crossed themselves. So did Idrun. From somewhere at the back came a sombre, tremulous voice:

'Not a cloud, friends, but a vision. It must have been the devil himself flying over our country, God save us—'

It took Idrun some time to find a trough in the yard of the hospice. The water looked muddy, no towel or napkin was provided, and Idrun had to dry his hands on the grass. It was a relief to hear Dom Paul call out to him:

'It is time we were off, my son.'

IX

Idrun's Triumph

Time did not pass for Idrun: it flew, and week by week, month by month, Dom Defensor knew that he had a prince among pupils in the boy. 'If there were more such in Frankland, the country will not perish,' thought the old man but, faithful to his duty, he seldom, if ever, praised Idrun who would be punished for the least slip in grammar, the least lack of punctuality, even for coming to the library, his hands unwashed and his hair untidy. Excuses meant nothing to Dom Defensor.

'Sir,' Idrun once pleaded, 'I helped Dom Paul to catch a fowl and I did catch it near a muddy puddle.' He added, 'Dom Paul said I could run like a deer!'

'There is plenty of water at the guest-house,' the old man said dryly.

'But if I'd stopped to wash my hands, I'd have been late.'

That was logic at its clearest and best, but Dom Defensor maintained that Idrun was at Ligugé to study and not to join kitchen brothers in chasing run-away poultry, and that day Idrun dined off stale bread and a cup of water.

He did not mind the punishment, and whistled as he washed the cup. He could find no words to explain it, but he felt as though he were a bird flying high among the clouds. He had mastered the alphabet within less than a week, and all but trembled with joy when at the end of the first month Dom Defensor taught him how to hold the style, dip it into the inkhorn very carefully—'No blots,' said the old man, 'parchment costs dear'—and, cheeks flushed, tongue licking his lips, began tracing his own name. The old monk watched him closely.

'It is a pity your name doesn't lend itself to a contraction,' was all he said.

Idrun stared.

'What is that, sir?'

'We'll come to it in good time.' Dom Defensor left his stool, stretched towards a shelf and, opening a large stoutly bound book, leafed it at random until his forefinger pointed at a word.

'Can you read it?' he asked.

Idrun stared. The word seemed to be nothing but consonants, here and there crowned by short horizontal lines. He shook his head.

'Sir, it looks like a riddle to me. Why, there is not a single vowel!'

'Don't you see the lines above? They are meant for the vowels.' Very slowly Dom Defensor read out the third word of the Lord's prayer in Latin—'hallowed'—'benedicetur'—which, an unknown scribe had turned into 'bn̄dc̄tr̄.'

'That is your contraction. We have to use many of them because of the scarcity of parchment.'

When grammar and calculus were done there followed the best time of all: the old monk, looking beyond Idrun into the cloister, would talk about all things under the sun. The way of the stars, the way of a seed buried in the ground, the tides and the winds, fishes, animals, stones, trees and plants, the entire chronicle of the earth seemed opened to Idrun, and he listened, motionless, his mouth slightly open, his grey eyes glinting with gold.

'Sir,' he asked once, 'you must have travelled far to know all these things?'

The old man smiled thinly.

'I came from a hamlet in Brittany to Ligugé. My father was a fisherman. What little I know I have learnt here—' and, as the bell broke across the garth, he said hurriedly, 'God go with you, son. Enjoy your dinner.'

Once only did Idrun see his teacher really angry, and it happened just before Berno's men were coming to fetch their master's son to Clear Water.

'I hope,' said Idrun, staring at the sunlit cloister, 'that we shan't
have to spend a night at Poitiers.'

Dom Defensor stared hard at him.

'You know that is out of the question, son,' he said dryly. 'Your
father's horses will be tired enough and none but a madman
would venture to ride through Mal Forest at night.'

'I loathe the Golden Grape. It is noisy and smelly, and men get
drunk there and they quarrel—'

'You need not go to the inn. There is St Martin's Hospice.'
Idrun said nothing.

'What is wrong with it? I am sure nobody gets drunk there.'
Idrun broke out:

'It is dirty and shabby and smelly. Those miserable pilgrims—'
he drew a breath—'look like so many starved dogs, and they are
fed like dogs. I have been there.' He went on passionately—'I
have seen it. I could smell the rotten fish and those men wolfed it
as though it was fine, roasted meat. They sat on the ground too.'
He stopped.

Dom Defensor had turned his face away towards the sun-
dappled garth. When he spoke his voice rang harsh:

'How often have you been to the hospice?'

'Once, twice, maybe,' Idrun answered grudgingly, 'and I never
want to see it again—and—'

But the old man would not let him go on. The stool creaked,
and Idrun shrank back from the anger in the sunken grey eyes.

'You've had your say, and I mean to have mine. By our rule,
the hospice is open to all men, no questions asked of them and no
money expected. Of the crowd you saw there, very likely, less
than ten were true pilgrims, resting on their way here. The rest
would have been idle vagabonds, serfs on the run, men who won't
work and expect others to pay for their laziness. When the hospice
was first opened, it had clean rushes on the floor, benches and one
long table. The visitors had proper meals well cooked, good pallets
to sleep on, plenty of fresh hay. By the end of the first week the
place looked as filthy as a neglected pigsty. And worse! They
had stolen everything—down to the last platter and the last iron

spoon. If they happened not to like a dish, they would throw its contents on the floor. I well remember the master's complaints to the lord Abbot who had nothing to say except that the brothers in charge should clean up the place. But the hospice has stayed open. All the dirt and the ingratitude mean less than nothing. We don't help them as them—but we answer the Lord's love in the best way we can.'

Idrun sat silent.

'Do you understand? I have made you read Pope Leo's book on charity. Did the words mean nothing? All the learning you get here won't be of much use to you if you close the door on charity.'

Idrun's cheeks were flaming by now. He hung his head.

'I see, sir,' he murmured under his breath, and got up on hearing a bell, 'and I shall remember it—always—'

Dom Defensor smiled.

When, in late August 731, Idrun rode to Clear Water, there to stay for some weeks and help his father with the harvest and the winter sowing, it was good to be back and he felt there had grown no gulf between the life at Ligugé and the pattern followed at Clear Water, and Idrun knew that his father realized it. For all Idrun's knowledge of Latin, arithmetic and other things, his hands had not lost their cunning with the axe, the harrow, the hatchet and the plough. Berno worked him hard enough, and few were the moments Idrun was able to spend with Gunto, to listen to the summer chronicle of the steading and to tell his friend about the life led at the Abbey.

Gunto marvelled.

'Saints be praised, Idrun, and I always thought that monks spent their whole days at prayer and rich guests brought them food and money—'

Idrun smiled. 'You should see them in the fields, Gunto! Every task you have learned at Clear Water is familiar to them, and for one meadow and wood of my father's they have ten or fifteen.'

At least one pleasant surprise awaited Idrun on his arriving at Clear Water that time. He had been hard at work in the bean fields all day and, trudging home, he realized that nearly a week had passed without his seeing Judith, nor had her name been mentioned by anyone. Was she ill? Was she—his heart gave something of a jerk as he ran into the hall and looked for Aldis. He found her seated at her spinning-wheel.

'Mother!'

Aldis looked up and frowned.

'Oh, son—you did startle me! What is it?' She glanced at his muddied legs and very dirty hands and added: 'You are not going to sit down to your supper in such a state! Have you been messing with the pigs or what?'

Idrun waved the question away.

'What have you done with Judith?' The words shot out like so many arrows. Aldis's finely moulded hands began stroking the spindle.

'What a bridegroom you'll make, son,' she said mockingly. 'Nearly a week at home and that is the first time you have noticed Judith is not here.'

'Where is she?' he cried, blood rushing to his face.

'At Troissant. She left the day before you came. That very old nurse of hers was dying. Of course, I told Judith she must stay for the funeral and the feast. Vorgis would not be much use to Master Turgot.'

'How is she?'

'Who?'

'Judith, of course.'

'There is nothing the matter with her except that training her in the ways of our house is wearing me to the bone.' Aldis slipped the spindle into the slot and sighed. 'She should have been born a boy. However, your father and I have come to a decision—'

'What?'

'You'll hear about it from Judith. She'll be at Mass tomorrow and coming back here. Mind, son, no quarrelling on the way home. We do need peace—what with the dreadful Saracens and

Saxons in the world . . . there is hardly any spice to be bought now—' She went on plaintively, 'I am sure I don't know how we'll manage come Christmas, and the price of leather is appalling, your father says.'

'But what is your decision?'

Aldis looked sly.

'Ah, that will be a surprise, Idrun.'

Next morning Idrun thought old Sir Martin would never finish his Mass. Not only was he slower than ever but, having ended one prayer, he would pause, and then start it all over again. In the end, his little congregation found themselves blessed precisely four times.

Idrun had seen Judith on coming into the chapel. With Vorgis just behind, Judith knelt by her father's side. She wore a plain blue gown Idrun had not seen before; her feet were bare but her hair seemed astonishingly tidy.

Once outside the little chapel, Idrun remembered his manners and bowed to Turgot. Then abruptly he turned to Judith and they kissed each other on the left cheek.

'I am told to walk back with you,' he mumbled awkwardly.

'Yes.'

So they waited in the sunlight for Vorgis and all the other Troissant folk to vanish to the left of the track. Berno, Aldis and Turgot and all the people from Clear Water turned right, and Idrun noticed the half-mocking glance thrown by Malina at Judith.

But at last they were alone. Even old Sir Martin had shuffled back into his hut to busy himself with his meal of eggs and porridge. To the right and the left of them, loud voices grew thinner. At their feet the stream ran its silver streak down into the valley, and the first tints of autumn on oak, beech and lime looked like so many jewels under the sun.

They moved on slowly towards the Clear Water lands. At last Idrun asked brusquely:

'Well, what's the surprise?'

'Hasn't your mother told you?' Judith parried without looking at him.

'She said you would.'

'Well,' she began, her head bent, 'they—I mean—your parents have decided—well—that things would go easier if I had one day out of seven all to myself.'

'What do you mean?'

'Well, do what I like—take a horse from the stables and ride all on my own, or walk, or do nothing at all—and your mother gave me a satchel to put the food in for the whole day—'

'And how many such days have you had?' Idrun asked grimly.

Judith laughed and sprawled on the very edge of the stream, her small, deeply tanned feet in the water.

'She should have been shod to go to Mass,' Idrun thought, but he did not say so.

'Just one.'

'And what did you do?' Now mockery crept into his voice.

'Do? Why, nothing. I had the day to myself and that was more than enough, and even Malina did not dare to interfere—' Judith stopped, but Idrun said nothing at all so she went on: 'I must be a nuisance at Clear Water—and yet I can't help it. All the needlework and the rest of it, and your mother doesn't under-stand—'

Idrun turned, his eyes aflame with anger.

'Don't you dare to say a word against my mother, do you hear?'

'But, Idrun, I was not saying it against her. You don't know how happy I feel for that gift of a day—' And Idrun's anger was shredded at Judith's adding: 'I did not deserve it—so many stupid things I have done.'

'They were not all stupid,' he muttered. 'I'd have put a dozen dead toads in Malina's bed.'

If Idrun had spent a whole week at home without asking after Judith, Berno did not seem to show any interest in Ligugé. His son was at home and would help with the harvest, and he understood from Aldis that the boy had been well bedded and boarded by the

monks. The rest was of no concern to Idrun's father. He had kept
his promise: the boy was getting what he wanted. Not until that
Sunday dinner did Berno ask:

'And what happened to that Judas of a prior, son?'

'He is not Prior any longer.' Idrun's eyes were on his platter.

'What is he then?'

'Helping Dom Tibo, the swineherd.'

The men burst into loud laughter.

'Have you seen him among the pigs?' Berno wanted to know.

'Once,' and quickly Idrun turned to one of the serving women
and asked for more beef.

After dinner, Turgot went back to Troissant. Berno made for
the orchard, there to sleep under a pear-tree. Judith vanished.
Aldis, Idrun and all the others were only too glad to observe the
customary Sunday ritual of a good long nap.

But that particular Sunday they were not to enjoy it. All
suddenly there was the steady beating of hoofs in the courtyard
and a stranger's loud, clipped voice summoning someone to hold
his horse. Within an instant Gunto came running to where Idrun
lay at the foot of the stairs.

'It's the Count's messenger—or a tax-collector,' he said,
shaking Idrun by the shoulder. 'I dare not wake the master.'

Idrun sat up and rubbed his eyes.

'It can't be . . .' he yawned, 'on a Sunday! No, no, Gunto, you
must not disturb my father.'

Here both boys heard the rustling of a woman's gown and
looked up. Aldis began going down the steps, and Idrun saw that
her lips were set and her face pale, but she held herself with dignity
and gave her orders to Gunto in a steady voice.

'Don't wake your master. Ask the gentleman to come in and
fetch a cup of beer and some wheaten bread.' Here she turned to
Idrun. 'Stay here, my son.'

They did not have long to wait. A portly man came in and
bowed to Aldis very politely. His green tunic was spotless and the
plaited thongs over his legs shone as though they had been greased
that very morning. An enormous leather pouch hung from a belt

studded with silver stars. But his eyes were small and his lips very thin. Idrun disliked him on sight.

According to custom, the visitor's business was not mentioned until he had eaten and drunk. Then the fat man leant against the wall, wiped his lips and fingers with a napkin, and drew a paper out of his pouch.

'I am here on the Count's business,' he said. 'Is the master away from home?'

'He is resting,' and Aldis added pointedly, 'today being Sunday.'

The Count's messenger bowed again. His podgy hands held an oblong piece of parchment. Idrun looked at it greedily.

'One such paper was sent to Berno in early summer. He took no notice of it. The Count does not like to have his messages ignored.'

'I know nothing about it,' Aldis said calmly. 'I do know that my husband pays all the taxes required of him.'

'It is not only about the taxes,' the man explained gently, 'but the muster in the spring.'

'We have paid for our exemption. Ah these wars! Whom have we to send? My husband could not leave the steading. We have not a single free-born Frank working on the land,' she repeated stubbornly, 'and we have paid for the exemption—'

'Three times over,' boomed Berno's voice from the threshold.

The fat man stood up and bowed, the piece of parchment fluttered down on the flagstones. Idrun stooped for it, glanced at the first line, and stepped back, the parchment still in his hand.

Berno ignored the bow. He came closer and towered over the unwelcome guest.

'If you were not under my roof, I would kick you,' he said levelly. 'What do you mean coming on a Sunday and at such a time of the year? I have never paid my exemption in August.'

'Times have changed,' broke in the Count's messenger, 'and there is a penalty for insulting my office.'

'I have not done so—'

'If you can't send anyone to join Duke Charles's army,' went on the fat man, 'it is your duty to help with the victualling. There is a special muster come Christmas.' He threw back his well-combed head and looked at his hands, then saw the piece of parchment still in Idrun's grasp, and spoke harshly. 'Come, give me the Count's order, boy—'

'Stay where you are,' Berno thundered at his son, but Idrun did not: he took a few steps back and began reading aloud:

'Three oxen, ten pigs, five horses, ten sacks each of meal, root vegetables and salted meat, five casks of mead—' Here he broke off and glanced at the foot of the sheet: 'Father, the order is dated back three years. It is not meant for Clear Water at all, but for someone south of Ligugé—' He panted and trembled, but the look Berno gave him was the greatest reward in his young life.

The Count's messenger, portly as he was, did not lack agility. He sprang towards Idrun, but Berno's arm shot out.

'Back,' he roared.

'That stripling,' cried the man furiously, 'he has made it up. For one like him to pretend to know his letters—'

Berno's enormous hand fell on the man's shoulder. He wriggled and struggled, but he could not get free of that iron grasp.

'That stripling,' said Berno in a dangerously quiet voice, 'is my son and the heir of Clear Water. He has learned his letters at Ligugé, and when he goes back, he shall carry this parchment to the Abbot. Ligugé has many wealthy tenants south of the Abbey, and—' Still clutching the man's shoulder, Berno flung at his son:

'What is the name, son?'

Idrun spelt it out.

'Elfon, Father. I have never heard of him.'

'I have,' Berno said grimly. 'You would not find a more honest man in the whole of Poitou. He works his lands with free-born Franks, and I happen to know that he had sent thirty of them to the muster three years ago, and this paper is about the victualling he had given. Insulted your office, have I?' he shouted. 'You are not fit to hold it, hound that you are, fouling the fair name of a Frank! How many farmers have you cheated with the same paper—ah—tell me that?'

He loosened his grip, and the fat man sank on the floor, his little eyes glazed with terror.

'Let me go. . . . Let me go . . .' he stuttered again and again.

'Let you go? Of course, and on a horse you must have stolen from some-one! Eh?' He shouted at the men who stood crowding outside the doorway: 'One of you run fetch an empty sack, fill it with pig fodder, and tie it to the saddle.'

Somehow quiet crept into the hall. Berno stretched himself full length on the nearest trestle and emptied a big horn cup full of beer. Aldis all but fell on a stool against the wall. Her face was flushed. Her eyes looked starry. She breathed:

'Oh, husband—there's one thing we forgot—to ask the rogue for his name.'

Before Berno could reply, Idrun's voice was raised:

'It's all right, Mother. It is in the paper.'

Berno refilled his cup and said awkwardly:

'Well, son, I was proud enough the day you killed that wild boar. I feel still more proud now—' and he laughed. 'Now let a tax-collector come to Clear Water once you are back home.'

From out of a shadowy corner Judith moved towards them and came close to Idrun.

'I'll never scratch or strike you again,' she whispered, and at once he turned on her:

'I don't want a milk cheese for a bride,' he muttered but his mouth was smiling—and the smile broadened when he heard Berno say:

'When you leave here, son, you shall take a message from me to that teacher of yours. It is time that wretched monk, Simeon, were relieved of his penance. I'll feel easier in my mind—somehow.'

'So shall I, Father,' Idrun answered.

X

The Hour of the Avalanche

That Christmas of 731 Idrun could not leave Ligugé. Even the way to Poitiers was more or less impassable because of the high snow-drifts, and the valley of Clear Water was virtually cut off. The oldest among the monks could not remember such snowfalls; the cold, having started at the end of October, grew so bitter that by November a small brazier had to be installed in Idrun's corner at the guest-house, but in spite of it, the ink often froze in the horn, and all the hurry of Dom Paul could not prevent Idrun's soup and porridge being coated with rime on the way from the kitchens. The rule had to be relaxed, and the monks fed in the infirmary, the only heated building, apart from the Abbot's lodging, in the whole of Ligugé.

All the Abbey lands slept under their thick blanket of snow. Cattle, pigs, horses and poultry were sheltered in byres, stables and sheds. Novices would be excused from devotional tasks to sweep narrow paths clear from one building to another, and Idrun, his own work finished, often helped them.

It was a strange, stilled, waiting world. When more and more snow fell, the flakes grew larger and thicker. One such fall just before Christmas brought down a whole row of thorns along one side of the kitchen-gardens. Often enough Idrun would come on birds lying motionless in the yards, the garth or elsewhere. No lowing of cattle was heard, as though the beasts themselves were stunned into silence.

The flagstones of the cloisters would often be coated with thin ice, and many a time Idrun would measure his length on his way to the library where the leather curtain was drawn, but not even a brazier was there to soften the day's rigour, and Dom

Defensor, huddling in a fur coverlet, would welcome him with a joke:

'Surely, this is better than an oven, son—'

'An oven, sir?'

'The infirmary,' explained the old man, 'is enough to roast a dozen bullocks. Well, do you mind this weather?'

Idrun did not. Even when his fingers were sore and numb, when the food he ate did not warm him, and the brazier's flame went

ashen grey towards sunset, Idrun felt at the very top of the world. Everything seemed right, and no winter lasted for ever. On his return he had told Dom Defensor about the visit of the Count's messenger and remembered Berno's message about Dom Simeon.

The old man laughed.

'Well done, Idrun. At least, your father won't think that you have wasted your time here! And for that man to use Elfon's name is just shameful.' His eyes ran quickly over the paper. 'Yes, yes, I will certainly take it to the Prior.'

Idrun ventured, 'And about Dom Simeon, sir?'

'That is not a matter to concern you.'

And then, all too soon, the cruel winter held the world in its grip. On the very bitter days Idrun was allowed to dine and sup in a corner of the kitchens. There were no visitors at the Abbey, but occasionally a monk or two would succeed in battling their way through to Poitiers. In the kitchens the brethren were allowed to speak about culinary matters alone, but little by little Idrun came to notice the growing exchange of uneasily whispered remarks.

'See that the porridge does not burn, brother. So, as you say, the Duke has ordered an extra large muster for Christmas?'

'Yes. . . . I believe the eggs are ready.'

'Surely he does not mean to fight during winter?'

'Fetch some more wood, brother. Fight? Nobody knows anything—but the muster is on. I have heard of a man who employs forty men on his land, and twenty-five of them have to go—ah—these hard times.'

'And whom would he fight? The Saxons again? Some salt, please.'

'The Saxons? The muster starts at Sens and goes on south—as far as Toulouse, so I heard—'

'And Poitiers?'

'Yes, there is to be one there. That I know for certain. I must have some more flour, brother. The broth is too thin.'

From his corner, head bent over his platter, Idrun heard it all. What did it mean? And Clear Water would be cut off. . . . He thought that the Clain must be frozen hard, but he supposed that the snowdrifts between Troissant and Clear Water would prevent anyone from fighting their way up and down the valley. He dared not ask questions from anyone in the kitchens. He was far too shy to approach the guest-master. But his teacher would surely enlighten him.

Dom Defensor did not.

'A muster at Christmas? That is not a matter to concern us here at Ligugé. We never meddle in the world's affairs. Where did you hear that gossip, my son?'

Idrun blushed. The old man rubbed his thin, blue-veined hands and shook his head.

'The saints preserve me from ever listening to such gossip,' he murmured. 'No, you are not to do any writing this morning. Your hands are so numb that a hare might use the style better.

Here is a homily of Pope Gregory on courage—read the first paragraph, will you?' and when Idrun had done, Dom Defensor smiled.

'Now you are going to have a treat—a poem by Fortunatus about the spring. I wish,' he sighed, leafing over a thick volume, 'I had lived in his time.'

'Was he a Frank, sir?'

'Indeed no. He came to our country from Italy more than a hundred years ago, and the blessed Radegund of St Cross befriended him. He died as Bishop of Poitiers. It is good to read him in these cruel, cold days—there is a breath of swelling bud and running sap in every line.'

Idrun duly read the poem, but its spirit escaped him. His mind was wholly absorbed in the kitchen gossip. Was Duke Charles getting ready to fight those same Saracens whom his mother blamed for the least disruption of the daily routine under the roof of Clear Water? Dimly he felt that something was about to happen.

Yet the blizzards soon put an end to anyone's excursions to Poitiers. There was no more gossip in the kitchens, and Idrun breathed more freely. It would be sad not to go home for Christmas, not to watch the gold-red flames leaping and dancing all over the huge Yule-log, not to exchange star-shaped pieces of gingerbread with everybody, the detestable Malina included, not to enjoy the traditional stuffed goose and honey pancakes and, worst of all, to miss the dancing and the singing which closed the happy, busy day. . . . Still, at Ligugé, Idrun had some gingerbread and a present of ten sheets of parchment from the Abbot. Dom Defensor put the neat parcel between Idrun's hands and said smilingly:

'Tomorrow I am going to deliver your father's message to the lord Abbot.'

Idrun blushed for pleasure.

Idrun was wrong in thinking that Clear Water was wholly cut off. Southwards, the track lay deeply buried indeed, but Turgot and Berno had all their men out to clear a path between Troissant and Clear Water. At Idrun's home, all the beasts and poultry were within the enclosure, and on Sundays when the household went to Mass, the gates would be heavily bolted and barred. The men, all of them carrying axes, walked in front and at the rear, the women between them. The precaution was more than ever necessary that winter: the howling of hungry wolves could be heard not only through the night but even by day-time, and the gates were guarded from sunrise to sunset. On one occasion, a careless youth would have been savaged by a wolf—had it not been for Grifo running to the rescue and killing the beast not a second too soon.

The steading would have been dark were it not for the huge fire, all the windows being shuttered. Wooden slats, nailed together, had replaced the leather curtain at the entrance. The upper chamber having no fire, Berno and Aldis slept below in the hall, and so did Judith, and the entire household since there was no means of heating their huts.

Clear Water looked like a jewel set in silver, but Judith saw its beauty in broken glimpses when she ran on some errand from the house to the dairies and back again. Grifo kept assuring his master that they had enough fodder to last till Easter, but the cattle found their confinement most irksome. The milk still given by the cows was so thin that even Malina's ingenuity could not turn it into cheese. For all the fodder they had, such of the beasts as were marked for slaughter provided coarse, stringy flesh lacking both savour and fat. There were no more eggs, and every morning Aldis and Malina went through the store-rooms, their eyes sombrely considering the half empty bins and shelves. Not all the barley and rye had been turned into flour; the nearest mill lay beyond their reach—nearly an hour's tramp from Troissant. Day by day, week by week, the diet grew more monotonous. The sameness would not have troubled the mistress of Clear Water: she felt anxious because hunting, the chief source of replenishing a larder in those days, was out of the question, and Berno kept saying that even his father could not remember a winter when the Silver Lake was frozen from end to end. You could run and dance on the ice, and it held you—not that anyone from Clear Water ever ventured so far.

Christmas passed, no merriment colouring the mood of anyone. Judith was at her worst. She laughed at all the precautions taken for their safety, and boasted that given a good weapon, she was perfectly able to forage for food on the wooded slopes of the hills.

'You have come here for your wedding, not your funeral,' Aldis snapped at her. 'Have you finished lining that wolf-skin I gave you?'

'Not yet,' pouted the child. 'It is hard work—sewing with the smoke in your eyes.' She added defiantly: 'Eggs are always scarce in winter, snow or no snow, but at home we never lacked fresh meat—'

'Your home is here,' retorted Aldis angrily. 'Fetch the wolf-skin at once, do you hear?'

And late into the night she would whisper her complaints to Berno.

'What shall we do with such an idle, improvident and hot-tempered girl in the family? Tell me, husband.'

'Ah, well, the winter won't last for ever,' Berno muttered sleepily, 'something is sure to happen, wife.'

And something did happen—just before Lent. There was a sense of mildness in the air and the winds no longer lashed like well-tempered steel. The frosts held on—but here and there along the path to Troissant the mounds of snow were no longer able to hold their own against the sun: they grew thinner and smaller. By contrast, the howling of wolves grew in volume; and when Sunday came, Berno announced his decision not to go to the little chapel.

'Nobody is to leave here. There is a whole pack of them prowling up and down.'

Yet a day or two later Turgot called at Clear Water. He vaulted over the high gate as though it were a wicket, and strode across the yard, his fur cloak open at the throat. When one of the men had pushed aside the slats by the entrance, Judith leapt to her feet, but Turgot brushed his lips against her cheek, his air preoccupied and, bowing to Aldis, made for Berno and whispered something un-heard by anyone else in the hall.

Berno raised his head, astonishment widening his blue eyes.

'Husband,' Aldis began, but he motioned her to be silent and led Turgot to a low bench at the farthest end of the hall.

Nobody spoke or moved. The master and his guest went on with their muttering. The great fire burned fiercely enough, but a chill threaded its way up and down the place. A sense of peril far greater than that of a wolf's attack came under the roof. At last, Berno rose and spoke in a loud, clear voice:

'No need to make a secret of it, neighbour,' and he came for-ward to face his household.

'Folks, Master Turgot has come to bring us some very grave news. A friend of his from Tours is now at Troissant, and Duke Charles's army is there—all in readiness to move South, the Duke's scouts having brought reports of an immense Saracen host standing at the very foothills of the Pyrenees. The passes are still dangerous, but those infidels mean to cross the mountains as soon as the snows are gone and bring fire and sword into our country.'

The women gasped and fell on their knees. The men crossed themselves. Judith's face went as grey as her smock. The towel she had been hemming slipped off her lap and covered her bare feet. Aldis stood up.

'Master Turgot,' she stammered, 'where will the Duke's men make for once they leave Tours?'

'Poitou and Aquitania.'

No man or woman at Clear Water knew much, if anything, of Aquitania, but they all belonged to Poitou, and Poitiers was a home word to them. Judith shivered, and raised a shaking hand to her lips, and Aldis, her face matching her white veil in colour, again fell on her knees.

'Mother of God, with Idrun at Ligugé!'

Berno said nothing.

'You will stay the night.' He turned to Turgot. 'Have you dined?'

Judith's father shook his head.

Berno shouted his orders. Food and drink were carried to Turgot.

'I have come,' he said, pushing away the emptied cup and trencher, 'to say good-bye. All my men, except three, and myself are joining the Duke's host. The ice on the Clain still holds, and we'll make for Bourges and Autun—' He smiled grimly. 'It will be a costly war for the country. Seventy-two horses and goodness knows how many cartloads of weapons and victuals are leaving Troissant, and a sack of money too. . . . Nothing is to be spared.'

'And you have walked here?'

Turgot shrugged.

'It is still too cold to ride, and—'

He was interrupted by Judith. She was up, her hands clenched together.

'Father, I must go back with you.'

'You are to stay here,' he replied harshly. 'Troissant is no place for a chit like you,' and the very tone of his voice made it clear to Judith that all further pleas would fall on stony ground.

The day died; the women prepared the guest's bedding and bustled about getting the supper. The men ate little and in silence. The night's prayers said, Berno ordered the rushlights to be put out, but few, if any, had a good night's rest at Clear Water. The men muttered as they tossed on the straw. The women smothered their sobs as best they could. Judith lay wide awake on her pallet and stared at the leaping flames on the hearth. An expensive war and a long one, her father had said. She thought of November and her wedding-day, and her little hands were cold under the fur coverlet.

Aldis fell into a fitful sleep, and woke several times, a grimly clear nightmare graven in her mind: Poitou in flames, crushed by the Saracen heel, Ligugé . . . her son . . . her son. . . . But, even when fully awake, Aldis lay quietly. The ghastliness of it all was too big to be seized detail by detail. She opened her eyes and saw the fire glancing up and down Berno's red tunic neatly folded on the trestle near their bed, and she shivered. They would not have Berno join the army moving against the Saxons. That was many years ago. Dimly Aldis remembered that they had thought him unable to move fast enough because of some injury to his right shin. But, surely, he was perfectly fit now, and she shuddered again and caught his whisper:

'Wife, I am not going unless the infidel reaches Poitou, and that is not likely to happen. I'll stay the King's man to the end, but I'll spare nothing. The goblets must go and the silver, and as many head of cattle as can be added to Turgot's train.'

'And you can have all my buckles and the turquoise belt,' she whispered back. 'Master Turgot said his party won't move out of Troissant until the snows are gone.' She paused and then asked, her voice tremulous: 'Husband, will the Saracens cross the Pyrenees?'

'Turgot says they can, but I am not sure. There are many wooded heights, and a very savage tribe lives there. They never descend into the passes to fight, so I have heard, but they hurl huge stones at anyone going through the passes.'

'If that is so, how can there be a war?' she wondered, and Berno was silent.

He had indeed heard about the savagery of the Basques. He had also heard enough about the incredible cunning of the Saracens who had cut through the whole Iberian Peninsula with the ease of a knife slicing a big cheese.

That long, hard winter told on Abbot Ursin's frailty. The brothers who looked after him kept his lodging as warm as he allowed them to; an improvised kitchen was set up in a corner of the outer room so that his food might be served hot. The old man did not go outside but whenever the sun happened to turn the snow-mounds into jewels, the Abbot would have one or two of his study windows unshuttered, saying that the fresh air, however cold, never hurt anyone. Still, Dom Leo, the elderly infirmarian, saw to it that an extra fur coverlet was spread over the Abbot's knees and a special cordial was kept on the shelf in the study. Abbot Ursin made no protest but all of them knew that he regarded all of it as unnecessary fussing.

The sun shone brightly on the day when Dom Defensor came to deliver the message from Clear Water.

The Abbot frowned.

'Master Berno is a good Christian,' he murmured, 'but I can't reinstate Dom Simeon as Prior.' He sighed. 'I should really have sent him to prison.'

The old monk waited, but Abbot Ursin seemed to have nothing more to say and Dom Defensor plunged in:

'Of course not, my lord, but Dom Simeon writes so well, and there is so much copying to get done.' He added apologetically, 'Little could be done now—with the ink frozen.'

'Well?'

The other hesitated.

'You have young Idrun to help you—'

'My lord, the boy could not go home for Christmas. As you know, he will be leaving earlier for Easter—in Passion week, I think.'

'Well?' Abbot Ursin's pale hands began smoothing a sheet of parchment.

'There is not much, if anything, that I could teach the boy, my lord.'

'But he has done well, hasn't he?'

'Never had I hoped to have such a pupil—quick, intelligent, never bored. He'll be leaving us some time in the summer, I suppose—he reads well, his script is excellent, and so is his arithmetic—'

Dom Defensor might have added that Idrun's chief interest was centred in the books of Isidore of Seville, particularly such as dealt with nature: trees, flowers, minerals, animals, water and fire and cloud. The old monk well understood the reason for it: Idrun's heart was so deeply anchored at Clear Water that the smallest detail about the growth of barley or a fish frisking in the Silver Lake stirred and held him.

'I see,' said the Abbot, 'but what are you going to do when the lad comes back after Easter? There'll be quite two or three months to fill.'

'I think,' Dom Defensor said slowly, 'that I could trust him to copy my anthology—with your approval, my lord?'

'Have you told him so?'

The old man shook his head.

'Yes, that would be good,' said Abbot Ursin. 'We could send a copy to St Denys. Now, there's the matter of Dom Simeon. What do you think I could do?'

'Once Idrun is gone,' Dom Defensor spoke steadily, 'Dom Simeon might be of use in the library.'

Abbot Ursin stared.

'You mean—with you?'

'Yes.'

'You ask me to do that when you know how shabbily he behaved?'

'We all serve the same Master, my lord—' the old monk spoke quietly—'and He forgives everything.'

'Very well,' breathed the Abbot, 'I will have it done once Idrun has left us. You certainly do serve the Master, brother.'

Early in Passion week Idrun left Ligugé for Clear Water, his old teacher having said that a great surprise would await him on his return after Easter.

It happened the very next afternoon when the Vesper bell began clanging shrilly all over the great Abbey. Dom Defensor put his books away and started looking for his cowl. He found it rather crumpled between a volume of St Augustine and a crock of freshly made ink. The monk pulled at the cowl and upset the crock, the ink bespattering his feet and the flagstones. He knelt, trying to mop up the mess with an old rag used for cleaning his styles, when he became aware of an abrupt, deep silence. The Vesper bell had stopped. He could hear no shuffling of feet along the west cloister.

'Now what could have happened?' Dom Defensor stood up and looked down at his ink-stained feet.

It seemed such an unfamiliar silence just as if some thousands of giant hands were stifling all sound in the place. And then within a few minutes the ringing of a different bell startled the old man.

'A chapter meeting instead of Vespers!'

Hurriedly he tidied himself, washed his hands in the trough at the corner of the cloister, and, hoping that none would notice his feet, made his way to the Chapter House. The urgent bell went on and on, and all the ninety monks of Ligugé were on their way to the octagonal grey and red building to the east of the basilica. There, in unbroken silence, they mounted a curving flight of stairs, entered the hall, took their places in strict accord with seniority, and sat still, hoods pulled over their foreheads. They got up when Abbot Ursin came in and took the tall, carved chair at the end of the room. His face looked sunken and grey, but his hands did not tremble, and his voice rang steady when he started intoning the usual prayer. That done, he motioned the monks back to their benches.

'Brothers,' he began in a firm voice, 'each of you shall say his Vespers privately after the chapter. I have called it because I have just had a messenger from the Priory at Saintes. The Saracen army has crossed the Pyrenees. More than that! They are advancing northward. Toulouse and Bordeaux are in flames. The message said it was clear that they mean to get to Tours and Orléans—and to Paris—and that means their passing through Poitou—'

Abbot Ursin stopped. The ninety men seemed carved out of black stone. Not a hand was clenched, not a stir seen up and down the narrow benches.

'We all know that Duke Charles ordered a special muster last Christmas. I understand that his host has left Tours and is moving southwards to offer battle. I know no more than that, my brothers, except that the Saracens show little mercy to any Christian. We carry no weapons—we can meet their onslaught with a cross and a prayer—and no more. I wish every brother to go about his appointed task and to pray to the Lord, His mother, and St Martin, our founder and protector. Our sacristy and crypt are full of great treasures. Our library has a number of rare books. I do not wish anything to be hidden in the ground, but I want you to tell me if you think otherwise.'

At once ninety voices replied in unison:

'We don't.'

'Thank you.' Abbot Ursin bowed to the right and to the left, and added, 'We shall pray for all men, women and children at Saintes and Angoulême—but let us remember that whether we live or die, we are in His hands.'

The chapter was over. No other bell would ring until supper, and the monks dispersed in silence. Dom Defensor crossed the great garth very slowly. Spring breaths were all round about him, but he seemed unaware of them. He passed the west cloister and did not go into the library. He made for the guest-house instead, his sandalled feet making scarcely any noise on the flagstones of the little yard, and his head bent. He passed by the kitchens where a number of monks had already begun preparing the supper. All was silent within.

The guest-house was cool and empty. More from habit than piety the old man crossed himself passing the great iron crucifix.

They had removed the wooden screen from Idrun's little corner, and Dom Defensor came nearer, his eyes almost hungrily observing every detail: the crimson coverlet neatly folded over the pallet, the low stool, the coffer, a pair of shoes standing on it, the little lectern, its few appointments clean and neat, and for the first time in his life the old monk wept. Then he removed the shoes and, raising the coffer lid, stared at the evidences of Idrun's happy sojourn under that roof: a tidily folded red tunic, a pair of linen drawers, a bunch of styles tied together by a thin leather thong, a few sheets of clean parchment, a spare candle, a small ivory comb and what few books the boy had been allowed to borrow from the library.

'He'll be safe enough in the valley,' murmured Dom Defensor, 'and I know we shall meet again in the Lord's own hall.'

Slowly he turned back to the west cloister and, once he found himself in the library, he knew he was spent.

'But my work is done,' he muttered, pulled out his anthology, and glanced at the beautifully penned preface. '. . . as a harbour to a mariner. . . .' Ligugé, his work, the old Abbot and Idrun were so truly his harbour.

The bewildering, anxious day drew to its close with the solemn ringing of the Great Silence bell. Dom Defensor had certain privileges; that evening he used one of them and did not follow the others into the great dormitory. There was much copying to be done and also the annals should have demanded his attention. But Dom Defensor, in defiance of the rule, was plunged into idleness.

It was boys of Idrun's quality who sustained the hope for a despair-driven world, scarred and fretted by all manner of violence —war, famine, lust of conquest, terrors of invasion. . . .

He sat, his head bent, when a hand touched his shoulder, and he struggled to his feet.

'You should be asleep, dear brother,' murmured Abbot Ursin. 'I am on my way from the Chapel of the Miracle, and I saw your candle.'

Dom Defensor knelt by his stool.

'I had tried to pray, my lord,' he murmured, 'for Ligugé and for my dear pupil.'

'Then let us pray together,' said the Abbot and knelt in his turn.

No words were spoken. When after a while, Abbot Ursin rose to his feet, the old librarian saw the deep sunken eyes go fiery.

'All shall go well with the lad, dear brother,' he said and left the library.

XI

An Enclosed World

Idrun had expected to leave Ligugé for Poitiers with two or three brothers for his companions. The evening before he had taken leave of his teacher and heard of a great task awaiting him on his return to Ligugé. He would not ask questions, but he had said:

'I trust it is something I can do, sir.'

Dom Defensor had smiled, given him the blessing, and stood near an arch of the west cloister, watching the boy cross the great garth. Evening shadows had begun to thicken and, turning round, Idrun could barely distinguish the bent-shouldered figure.

It was Dom Alexis who woke him at dawn.

'Get up, son. Your father's men are waiting for you.'

'My father's men.' Idrun sat up, rubbing the sleep out of his eyes. 'Why should they have come here?'

The guest-master did not reply. Idrun dressed hurriedly, folded away what gear he was leaving behind, said a brief prayer, and ran into the yard. In the pearly grey light he saw Grifo and three men. They had not dismounted, and one of the men held Idrun's pony by the bridle. Greetings and farewells were exchanged, and at once Idrun knew that something was the matter. The men avoided his eyes and Grifo looked almost as miserable as though his saddle were covered with nettles. Idrun asked quickly:

'Are my parents all right?'

'Yes,' Grifo answered.

'And Mistress Judith?'

The foreman nodded.

'Any sickness among the cattle?'

'No, Master Idrun. Everything is in good trim at Clear Water.'

'Then why,' the boy demanded, 'do you look as though

a wolf were leaping at your throat?'

Grifo did not answer. Idrun shrugged. Once past the great Abbey gates they took the road towards Poitiers.

'I suppose we spend the night at the Golden Grape?'

'No, Master Idrun.'

The boy frowned.

'I'd much rather keep away from that hospice.'

Grifo said nothing. To Idrun's bewilderment, the foreman rode a little way ahead and turned away from the road to a very narrow uphill track. Idrun caught up with him soon enough.

'That is not the way home.'

'It is,' Grifo replied without turning round. 'Those are Master Berno's instructions. Mind your pony does not slip on the way up.'

'But where are we stopping for the night?'

'At the Ring of the Little Oaks. It is all arranged. Hamo is expecting us.'

Idrun's bewilderment deepened. He had never seen the Ring of the Little Oaks, a small and poor steading hidden among the larches at the foot of the mountains. But he had heard enough about it for the prospect to displease him. Hamo was someone's tenant, an uncouth, dirty man in the late fifties. Of substance he had little: a small patch of arable, a couple of pigs, a cow and a few hens. Willa, his wife, was suspected of witchery: she had been known to make a broth of nettles, hens' entrails and crab apples, muttering spells all the time. Once, as Idrun had heard, she had carried a crock filled with the concoction and poured it out in a field at some distance from their steading, and that farmer had lost nine head of cattle within a week, the muttered spells, so folk argued, having put poison into the broth. Idrun remembered the story and crossed himself.

'Hamo's wife is a witch.'

Grifo heard and did not reply. He had been ordered by Berno to keep away from Poitiers where wide, deep ditches were being dug all round about the city and where the mood of the people was fear, verging on panic: everybody had heard about Saintes and Angoulême. Nobody knew why Duke Charles's army seemed at such a standstill. At every corner in Poitiers people would gather and darkly hint at treason.

'I don't want my son to be disturbed by all that foolish talk,' Berno had said to Grifo. 'He would have heard none of it at the Abbey. I've no great love for monks, but, at least, they don't gossip.'

Grifo had no choice but to obey the instructions. He had been to Poitiers a week before to do some shopping for his mistress; he had heard much wild talk, and his own mind was filled with unease. Why did the Frankish army not hurry south and check the enemy's progress? Was it true that Duke Charles had accepted two cart-loads of gold and silver from the Saracens? Was there anything in the story about him turning infidel? Grifo could not tell.

It was hard going for the horses. The track wound up and up— in places it was so narrow that lichen-covered branches of old limes all but blinded the riders. And there seemed a peculiar stifling feeling about the place as though the very air had been sucked away. They could see little ahead except more and more trees and, high above, the grim slate-coloured heights of the mountains.

'We'll soon be there,' muttered Grifo, 'and when we leave the steading, we turn east and the going will be much easier.'

The Ring of the Little Oaks certainly justified its name: about a dozen or so of stunted, gnarled oaks stood about to the right and left of a miserable wooden hut, its entrance the only means of light. The steading breathed of poverty, neglect and dirt. The little yard had rotten vegetables for carpet; the none too fat pigs were lying under the oaks, and somewhere behind the hut the cows were mooing. Idrun, still in the saddle, stared at the two bent figures appearing round the corner. Both had wildly matted hair, dirt-grooved faces and toothless mouths folded in a grin meant for welcome. Idrun had heard of such people but he had never met them before, so sheltered a life had he led. He leapt down from the saddle and answered the grin with a smile. They bowed and made way for him. The little hut had no furniture except a single trestle, and hens' droppings littered the floor. But the narrow trestle was set forth with the best they could offer—a shapeless loaf of rough barley bread, some bitter beer in a crock, boiled turnips and a large pastry, blobs of congealed fat studding it. Hamo and Willa said little enough and Idrun could not grasp the dialect, but Grifo understood it, and his eyes brightened. The Ring of the Little Oaks knew nothing and cared nothing for the outside world. They had indeed heard of something about to happen—far away from their steading and of no concern to them. But they were free-born Franks and they urged their hospitality on Idrun who drank the bitter beer and struggled with the pastry. They had killed one of their chickens to make it, said Hamo to Grifo; and they had enough fresh hay for the young master's bedding, added Willa.

They left the little steading early at dawn. It was a gratefully cool morning, and it was good to be riding home. The track widened and widened. To the south Idrun saw the dark dim mass of Mal Forest. To the north loomed the mountains, graced by the morning sun, and within an hour they were riding along the familiar track to Clear Water. Idrun ventured:

'How dreadfully poor they are! How do they manage?'

Grifo bent over his saddle.

'Poor, young master? There are thousands of them in our country—Hamo is just feckless, to my mind, and she is worse! That woman knows less of housekeeping than a worm in the ground. I heard some folks say they had killed a pig last summer! I ask you!' Grifo sighed. 'Of course, the meat went rotten. . . . And that tattered smock Hamo wore! I shouldn't think she's washed it once since she made it. Poor soil, small steading and all, they'd no business to turn it into a pigsty—'

Grifo went on chattering about such things. He would not tell Idrun what Hamo had said to him:

'Some folks came here from Poitiers and they said the infidels were in the country. Well, it makes no odds to me. We could not be worse off than we are.'

They turned a bend in the track and the familiar landscape came into view, with the deep shadows of Mal Forest well to the south from them and the ever-widening track fringed by the rippling brook and the faint gold of the willows, winding up northwards.

'Come on, Master Idrun,' said Grifo. 'Such a surprise you'll get at home.'

But the surprise came some time before they reached the gates of Clear Water. Idrun knew it was his home. He could hardly recognize it. For the familiar double hedge he saw a tall wooden stockade, all the vertical planks reinforced by three rows of horizontal ones, with wickedly sharp iron spikes studding the top. The stockade seemed to enclose the whole of the manor, and Clear Water suggested a fortress rather than a private dwelling. Even the gates looked different: the stout oak had all but vanished under broad swathes of iron, and the top of the gateway now carried a double row of spikes. Idrun reined in and sat at gaze, his grey eyes growing wider and wider.

'It is a surprise indeed,' he cried angrily just when one of the men started fumbling for the horn tied to his saddle. 'What has my father been at?'

'He'll tell you soon enough; and that is not the surprise I meant,' retorted Grifo.

The horn sounded three times, and it seemed to Idrun as though the gate refused to let them in. He could see nothing, but excited voices reached him mingled with a perfect cacophony of sound— wood against iron and iron clanging against wood. Was Mal Forest teeming with starved wolves? he wondered, but Clear Water and its people knew how to meet that menace. There had never been iron spikes and . . . Here came more shouting from beyond the gate, something heavy toppling on the ground, and an iron bar slipped out of its slot, leaving the gate open. Idrun rode into the yard where the sense of the unfamiliar at once smote at him.

Pigs and poultry never before allowed in the courtyard were all over the place. A huge stack of logs usually kept at the back now filled one of the corners. Not a barn or a stable but had iron spikes on the roof. The whole place spoke of a frenzied determination to withstand an assault and to undergo all the hardihoods of a siege.

Berno was there, and Aldis, too. She rushed forward without giving her son time to dismount and kissed him as violently as she had done once before. Idrun blushed, stuttered something in- audible, and was relieved to hear his father's voice:

'Now leave off fussing him, wife. He is home. Nothing else matters.'

Grifo leapt out of the saddle and whispered to Berno:

'He has heard nothing at all, master.'

Like lightning across a summer sky came the memory of gossip once heard in the Abbey kitchens. Idrun stood and stared at his father.

'So the Saracens have crossed the Pyrenees?'

'Crossed the Pyrenees, son? Why, they have ravaged the whole of Aquitania. They may be in Poitou by now—but we know nothing at all except that the Duke's army is still to the south of Tours. If those devils find our little valley, Clear Water will give a good account of itself—' Berno gestured towards the gates already closed. Some six or ten men were clamping huge iron bars from the top to the bottom. 'Yes,' said Berno, 'I can't fight, and the Count won't take freed serfs . . . but at least we can defend one small corner of Poitou!'

Blood rushed into Idrun's cheeks.

'But I can fight, Father. Why, I am nearly fourteen—'

'Your business is to stay here,' thundered Berno, 'and defend your inheritance! Do you imagine that all my men and I have gone to all that trouble for nothing? You are much too young! One look from the Count, and you'd be sent home.'

Berno drew a breath, his eyes angry. Aldis and all the others kept silent. A pig snorted somewhere as though in contempt of Idrun's wild ambition, and he stood, his head hung low. 'What a home-coming,' he thought, 'and I am sure Judith will laugh at me. I am sure there are lads of my age gone from Troissant. Father is unjust. . . . If I am old enough to get married, surely I am old enough to fight for my land. . . .' His mouth shaking a little, he raised his head and looked round about him, but Judith was not to be seen.

The long and thorny pause was broken by Grifo clearing his throat.

'Master,' he ventured, 'I have told the young master there is a surprise waiting for him—'

'I have had it,' Idrun muttered in a colourless voice.

'And he does not deserve it,' shouted Berno, but Aldis stepped forward, her great eyes full of tears.

'Now, husband, that is more than enough. Can't you see the boy's mind is all in a whirl? What with the iron bars and spikes and the dreadful Saracens, it is peace we need here.' She added, 'And food, too—I am sure he got nothing but rotten turnips for his dinner yesterday. That Willa would not know how to roast an egg.' Aldis went on talking of wispy inconsequential things, and somehow the tension slackened. Men and women moved away to their work, the angry darkness left Berno's eyes, and Idrun let his mother seize his right hand.

'I have had my surprise,' he repeated awkwardly, and Aldis smiled through her tears.

'You don't even know what it is,' she said and clutched his hot hand. 'You must be pleased with it, son. It was your father's idea, and Judith helped, too.'

'And I have brought no gifts either for you or for her,' Idrun muttered.

'We don't need presents, lad. It is more than enough to have you back.' Here Aldis turned and looked at Berno who nodded.

'Take the boy along, wife.'

They moved towards the stables and behind them rose Malina's shrill voice:

'Mistress, ah, mistress, shall I start on the pancakes now?'

Aldis made no reply. She walked on, her head and shoulders erect, and she had the air of someone to whom common domesticities meant less than a shrivelled leaf. They passed the stables, the row of workshops, the beehives. The white roseate foam of the orchards in blossom gleamed here and there in between the pale golden buds of old limes, and Aldis stopped abruptly:

'Look to your right, son.'

Idrun turned. A small building, no bigger than a swineherd's hut, stood against the blind wall of the manor. The low roof was thatched, and to the left of the entrance was a square window.

Idrun gasped. 'It was not here in the autumn,' he cried. 'It is new . . . Is it another workshop, Mother?'

Aldis nodded.

'In a way it is. Go and see for yourself, son.'

Idrun ran, reached the threshold, halted and gasped. The place was small indeed. It breathed of freshly planed timber and rushes spread on the floor. Facing him was a pallet covered with a red-lined bearskin. A small crucifix, the ivory gone honey-golden with age, hung on the roughly timbered wall. To the left, nearest to the window, stood a low lectern, writing materials spread tidily inside the groove at the top. Above on a carefully planed shelf lay a heap of blank parchment sheets neighboured by a bunch of styles and an inkhorn. A low stool was placed in front of the lectern, and an oak coffer at the foot of the pallet completed the furnishings.

Idrun stood rooted, his eyes racing from one detail to another.

He went in, touched things, felt the softness of the coverlet, passed a burning palm across the cool wood of the lectern, saw a tall iron stick with a long tallow candle stuck into it, and his eyes went misty, but he felt no shame.

He turned to see Aldis in the doorway.

'It is all yours, son'—she spoke softly—'for leisure and for work. Your father thought you should have some reward. Gunto laboured over the furniture, and Judith rode to Troissant as soon as the snow had gone to fetch the parchment and all the rest. Are you pleased?'

Unable to speak, Idrun nodded. He had expected a welcome. He had never expected to be made master of that tiny kingdom.... The surprise of it all at once gladdened and shamed him. At last he found his voice:

'Pleased? Oh, Mother—this is Paradise.' He bit his lip. 'And where is Judith?'

'Somewhere in the garden—sewing, I think. We are all very busy, Idrun.' Aldis struggled against spoiling his pleasure and failed most dismally. She went past him into the hut, flung herself on the pallet, and sobbed:

'It is all dreadful, son. And you know nothing except what Grifo had heard. Poor Poitiers is deeply ditched all round, but they say the Saracens ride horses which can leap across the widest ditch, and they look like devils, son, so I heard, all smothered in white linen, their faces black-brown and their eyes—so many live coals. They use wickedly sharp curved swords in battle, and their horses run like the wind.' She wiped her face with the hem of her grey gown and went on: 'I dare not say so to your father, but if those devils do find this valley, no iron spikes will prevent them from rushing in . . . and it is dreadful to live without Mass—'

'Has Sir Martin gone, then?'

'No, but your father won't allow anyone to leave the steading. . . . Oh dear saints,' Aldis moaned, 'no fresh fish or meat . . . your father says it may last for a year—'

'But, surely, we'll fight them in the summer, Mother. Whoever heard of a war in the winter?'

'We know nothing at all. We can't even tell where our army is—' She sat up, rearranged her veil, and wiped her face again. 'Now—see—what a mother you've got,' and she smiled thinly, 'so to spoil your pleasure.'

'You have not spoilt it, Mother,' Idrun broke in, and he meant it.

She rose, and he saw how tired she looked.

'It hasn't been an easy winter for any of them here,' he guessed, and said aloud: 'Of course, it will be like a holiday—reading and writing here. Father will never have to complain that I neglect the outside work.'

'And there is so much of it,' Aldis murmured, and went.

Idrun had hardly taken in that small corner of Eden when a shadow fell across the threshold. Her legs and arms stained with damp soil, her hair as wild as ever, her grey smock patched most unskilfully, Judith stood, a basket of roots in her hands.

'Well, master scholar,' she said mockingly, 'I suppose you are going to miss all the meals now that you've got this, and you won't miss much, I tell you—'

'What a welcome!' he retorted, folding his best tunic into the coffer, and remembering the girl's share in it all, added awkwardly, 'Good of you to give me so much parchment.'

Judith's mouth curved in a sly smile. 'Oh! Father will never miss it—'

'You mean—you stole it?'

'There was nothing else I could give you;' and she added, 'Don't look so fierce, Idrun. I'll tell him as soon as he gets back—'

'How long were you at Troissant?'

'A couple of days. Mistress Aldis insisted on my getting back here, and I was glad, Idrun. That old Disul and his strawberries—'

'Strawberries?' He stared.

'Yes; he kept talking of a huge field with strawberries the size of a big apple, and they kept growing and growing, and the sky was all thick clouds. Troissant is no place to be in without Father. Vorgis kept crying out that Disul meant blood and not strawberries.... She wanted to come with me, but Mistress Aldis would not have it. They'll be safe enough at Troissant—' She swung the basket from her right arm to her left, put out a very pink tongue, and ran back to the kitchen-garden.

It was the strangest time in his life, those summer months of 732. Not a traveller or a pilgrim passed up or down the valley. Clear Water was enclosed indeed, all the livestock and the poultry gathered in. There were twenty-seven mouths to feed twice a day, and Aldis and Malina held interminable conferences about the diet. Salt and spices were doled out on Sundays only. The two women watched the fruit-trees most anxiously and, as the summer drew on, not a single windfall was allowed to rot. Hay for the pallets, earlier changed twice a month, now had to serve much longer since all of it meant fodder for the beasts. Cows meandered in and out from one little meadow to another, but grass grew thin and sparse. Aldis's little herb-garden suffered much from the drought fallen in July, but Berno would not allow any watering. The great well behind the manor had never let them down before, but the conditions were so strange, he argued, that the devil might all too easily put a curse even on the well. At the back of the orchard, the pond was dried up. Morning and evening they prayed for a good storm and a welcome downpour, but the skies remained stubbornly clear, and the sun looked an enemy.

Clear Water was not small; it had afforded plenty of space for its people, but now, shut off from the woods and meadows beyond the barred gate, all of them saw themselves as prisoners. Sour looks were seen and harsh words heard from sunrise to sunset. Aldis beat Malina for dropping an egg. The wife of the swineherd, caught helping herself to an unripe apple, was denied both dinner and supper that day. Idrun got the worst beating of his life the day he tore a leather thong when trying to get through a thorn hedge behind the dairy. Judith's eyes were often red-rimmed, but he asked no questions.

The little paradise of a hut brought him but little pleasure through those sultry days. For one thing both Berno and Grifo worked him hard. Enclosed and grimly fortified, Clear Water demanded much labour. The kitchen-garden, the orchards, the cattle, pigs, poultry and horses, everything within the stockade asked for more and more work. At dinner and supper, Aldis, anxiously watching the meagre portions laid on the platters, complained that she was getting short of unguents and cordials.

'I am sure Dame Melita would give me all I need,' she grumbled the day the swineherd had hurt his right arm and she, always proud of her skill, had to contrive a nettle bandage for him.

Idrun heard and all but choked trying to swallow his portion of unseasoned meat. Dame Melita was at Poitiers, and down to the south lay the beloved Ligugé. He felt sure that the monks were still out in the meadows, the fields and the woods. The life at Clear Water grew into a nightmare and supper over, he slipped to his hut, to think of Judith crouching in a corner of the hall and weeping because there was no news of her father, no news of anything. They were enclosed in a world they had not known before. Even Gunto, Idrun's closest friend, now seemed a stranger, his eyes clouded and his mouth set.

And there was no news at all. For all they knew, the whole country was overrun by infidels slaying and burning everywhere. . . .

Things eased a little in mid-August when the weather broke. For three days and three nights the rain came down in bucketfuls, and when it left off, Idrun knew he could breathe again. Ducks and fowls made for the pond brimful of water. The well was all right. The troughs were full, and the women were allowed to wash the clothes stiff and stained with the sweat of many weeks. The morning Idrun was able to splash the cool water all over his body, he felt reborn, and it was pleasant to see Judith, the dirt washed off her face and neck.

They reached the autumn in high heart—and that in spite of their knowing nothing. Two cows calved successfully, and they had fresh meat for their Michaelmas dinner. The nut trees ripened, and what berries there were, were gathered in. The days grew shorter, and Berno's men were busily sawing the logs for the fire. At supper, Aldis would not allow rushlights, and the scanty food was swallowed in the fitful light of the hearth flames. Idrun would

watch Judith, her head bent over her platter. He knew she was
fretting about Troissant and Turgot, and Idrun did not know how
to comfort her. What was happening to Duke Charles's army?
And Ligugé? Dom Defensor, was he all right. And poor old Sir
Martin? Had he enough kindling in his hut? Idrun rather doubted
it.

Aldis and Malina never talked much except about domestic
matters, but when one golden October morning, with the smoke
of bonfires spiralling up to the blue cup of the sky, Idrun made for
the kitchen-garden, he found a pigeon lying among the wheat
stubble in his mother's little garden. He stooped. It felt still warm
but it was dead and incredibly thin, hardly any flesh on the roseate
breast. He stood, holding it; when Aldis's voice made him turn
round:

'It is dead.' Idrun spoke in a hollow voice. 'Exhaustion, I think.
If only birds could speak.'

Aldis came nearer and touched the sunken breast.

'It must have flown a great distance, son.'

'Yes,' he murmured, and thought to himself, 'Did it come from
the south? Did it fly over Ligugé?'

'Put it on the bonfire, Idrun.'

He shook his head.

'I'd like to bury it. May I? Close to the pond. Such a small body,
and the soil is so damp we can grow nothing there.'

'Have it your own way.' Aldis crossed her arms and looked at
the dead bird. 'Only a pigeon, son, but also another victim of those
infidels.'

Idrun laid the little body on the ground, and went to search for
Judith and to fetch his spade. He found her in the stillroom, sorting
out the apples. He explained nothing. She slipped out and followed
him. He liked her silences. She held the pigeon now and left the
digging to him. Afterwards Idrun said awkwardly:

'Thank you.'

'Why? I have done nothing.'

'You did not chatter.'

'Well, it was a funeral, wasn't it?' She hesitated. 'Idrun, I suppose there are many places like Clear Water, some larger, some smaller, and all shut in, and for how long?'

Idrun could not tell her.

'I hate war.' She stamped her foot.

'We can't even tell if there is a war.'

'We've heard more than enough. Last night your mother had a dreadful dream about crowds of riders swathed in white, and smoke and fire, and their swords whistling. She said she heard women wailing and children crying. Why, Idrun?'

'Why what?'

'These ceaseless wars,' she shouted at him, and he shrugged.

'You are a Frank's daughter. You are betrothed to a Frank. You should not ask such stupid questions. Anyway, fighting is not a girl's business.'

'Isn't it?' retorted Judith, and hit Idrun hard.

But this time he did not strike back. He could not agree with her, and yet it seemed true enough: there was so little, if any, sense in war. . . . The brothers at Ligugé would never fight, he thought.

Aldis could not forget her dream. When she lay still at night, she imagined those terrible riders crashing into the yard and killing the peace of Ligugé with their wild, alien shouts. She had told Judith and Malina but not her husband who, Aldis felt sure, would have dismissed it all for a piece of feminine nonsense.

But the nightmare did not leave her even by daytime. She stopped scolding and punishing. She merely shook her head when Judith broke a comb.

'Your mother,' said Judith to Idrun, 'is not herself these days.'

'None of us are.'

Fear was the only reality left to Aldis, and anxiety the only seasoning for the day's dullness. The others did not share the fear. They certainly shared the anxiety, and they reached the end of October, a strangely sour mood gripping them. They were so hungry for news, and none came. It needed but a few days to All Saints' Tide, but they all knew there would be no wedding.

One morning, when everybody was about their business, and Aldis, helped by Malina, was weighing out the flour for the dinner broth, the sound of hoofs was heard outside. Aldis, her face as white as snow, clutched Malina's shoulder, and her voice came in a broken whisper:

'They are coming... they are coming. . . .'

'Now, now, mistress,' Malina whispered back, her own legs trembling for fear.

The sound drew

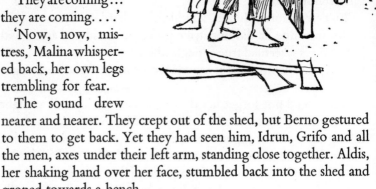

nearer and nearer. They crept out of the shed, but Berno gestured to them to get back. Yet they had seen him, Idrun, Grifo and all the men, axes under their left arm, standing close together. Aldis, her shaking hand over her face, stumbled back into the shed and groped towards a bench.

'Idrun, too . . . my son, my child. . . . They'll have no mercy on him—'

'Now, now, mistress,' murmured Malina, 'it is on our knees we should be and praying for God's mercy.'

At that very moment a different sound broke upon them: a horn was blown three times and then a familiar voice shouted lustily:

'Now then, neighbour! Tell your men to open the gate! I bring good news and I trust you can give a good dinner to five hungry men.'

'It is Master Turgot!' gasped Malina. 'Come on, mistress.'

Hand in hand they ran towards the yard where, axes on the

ground, six of the men were already grappling with bolts and bars. But the women did not run fast enough: a streak of grey rushed past them, and within a few seconds Judith was among the men, her strong, thin arms pulling at one bar after another, and when the gate screeched and was flung open, Judith rushed forward, her nails and palms stained with blood. She pressed her hot face against the flank of her father's horse. She seized his huge hand and, her wild hair pushed back, she covered that rough hand with her kisses until Turgot wrenched it away.

'Come on, daughter—' his voice rang harsh but his mouth was smiling—'the men are tired and hungry. Let us ride in.'

Judith stepped back. One of Berno's men ran up. The rest just stood and stared until Berno's voice boomed:

'And what is the good news, neighbour?'

Turgot dismounted, and said unhurriedly:

'There has been a great battle, Berno—' He stopped, and Berno urged him—

'Well? Where? What?'

'The infidels are beaten. They are on the run, over the Pyrenees by this time, I think.' He drew a deep breath. 'I am thirsty, Berno.'

Someone hurried forward with a jug of rosemary beer, and Turgot emptied it in three gulps.

'They'll never dare poke their noses into Frankland again. Oh—but it was a battle—'

Aldis came forward. She was no longer trembling.

'Come inside,' she said briefly, and led him into the hall. More beer was brought, and Turgot gave her a grateful look.

'Were you there?' shouted Berno, but Turgot did not answer him at once: one hand on Judith's tangled hair, he looked towards the entrance, saw Idrun, and smiled at him.

'Yes, I was there. Thirty of my men had gone with me to join the Duke's host, and five came back. God give peace to the others.' He made the sign of the cross, and lifted the mug to his lips. 'Where, did you ask, Berno? In the plain to the north of the Clain. The road to Tours lay open—and then Orleans and Paris. . . . The Duke would not move. We stayed in the camp through the whole summer, and oh, the drought. . . .' Turgot took another sip of the rosemary beer, and went on, 'Then the Saracens got tired of waiting. They wanted Paris; and they moved nearer—like a grey-white cloud, all of them mounted, the curved swords flashing in the sun, but we had our orders—and we stood still. And that—' here Turgot knit his eyebrows—'that, I think, lasted for a whole week. I can't rightly remember. . . . A holy relic was carried about, and we did not forget to say our prayers; and at night sentries kept on guard: then one morning—' here Turgot shuddered—'the Saracens moved forward—but they could not move our men. The business lasted from sunrise to sunset, so folks said, but I can't remember. . . . When a Frank fell, another leapt into his place, and our axes proved far more deadly than their swords. . . . It was all blood, and blood, and blood, but we stood our ground all right, and that, I now think, scared the infidels. When night fell all was still. At dawn we moved on and found their silken tents deserted. . . . I heard there was much treasure. . . . They rode back far more rapidly than they had come.' Turgot paused. 'I know no more. I came here at once—' he lowered his voice—'I fear it was a dearly bought victory.'

They had listened in silence. Then, at a sign from Aldis, the women began preparing a meal, and Berno led the guests to the great trough there to wash the dust off their hands and faces. Once inside, beer and bread were set out on the trestle, and Judith, her radiance a little dimmed, went and sat down in her usual corner.

Everybody knew that Turgot had much more to tell them, but his last words, 'I fear it was a dearly bought victory', seemed to have sealed their lips. The enemy had run away; the dearest friend was back among them, and they feasted him with the very best they could offer, but a breath of chilly quiet moved up and down the hall.

Idrun, his chin propped in both hands, sat motionless. Was Ligugé all right? He dared not ask.

EPILOGUE

A Curtain Rose and Fell

Turgot and his men left Clear Water the following morning. It was cold, grey, misty; Berno's household watched the guests vanish up the track, men shouting and women clapping, but Idrun, his own farewells made, went to his little hut and sat on the trestle. It was cold; he had no means of heating, but everything seemed dead to him, and when Judith slipped in, he would not raise his head.

'Your father's given everybody a day's holiday,' she cried. 'Oh, Idrun, your mother says Sir Martin will marry us before Advent.'

He did not answer.

'If we had bells here,' she went on, 'they'd be rung all day long. I suppose there is a carillon going on at Tours and Orléans.'

Idrun clenched his fists.

'Your father might have told us more. Just the battle and the Saracens' flight, and all the booty left to us. As though that were everything.' He spoke bitterly.

'What more did you expect?' Judith flashed at him. 'My father never repeats gossip.'

'He called it a dearly bought victory—'

Judith drew her brown woollen cloak close to her shoulders.

'No victory is cheap.' She raised her voice to a shout. 'And you look like an old woman robbed of a meal! Come to the house! It is so cold. I'll race you back!'

But Idrun did not move. When Gunto came to call him to dinner, he said piteously:

'Gunto, I beg of you—have you heard any more?'

'Plenty,' Grifo's son muttered, 'and so much is idle talk.'

'What of Ligugé?'

'Some say one thing—some another,' Gunto mumbled. 'But promise you won't give me away.'

'Never.'

'The master has just told us we'd be journeying south to-morrow. My mother's got some stomach trouble, and the mistress has nothing left in her medicine chest. So, it is Poitiers, Idrun, and I dare say the master won't grudge the time to get to Ligugé—'

Idrun's face brightened.

'So everything is all right there?'

'It sounds like it,' Gunto said and pulled his friend off the trestle. 'It is pork with roast apples,' he said, licking his lips, 'and the mistress does not want you to sit in here in the cold.'

'Is my father taking me with him?'

'Of course—but that is to be a surprise, Idrun. We go to the Golden Grape and then to that old man for you to buy a bridal gift for Judith, and the mistress needs spices, unguents and what not. That means St Cross. Thank heaven—the master is not taking any women with him. . . . The nuns would never chatter to us.'

To the end of his life Idrun would remember that journey; and the mild winds, the smiling blue sky did nothing but enhance the ghastly evidences of war. Sword and flame did not spare Poitiers. The Golden Grape was burned down—except for the cellars where Grafo, a thin shadow of a man, offered them what hospital-ity he had, and yet in spite of it all the bells would have rung at Poitiers if there had been any belfry left. St Cross Abbey was in ruins, but the ladies, so Grafo said, had taken refuge in a priory far to the east of Poitiers. St Martin's Hospice reared its gaunt charred skeleton to the cloudless sky, and yet what people were left in the town seemed all on fire with pride.

'No Saracens will ever dare to trouble the Franks again!' said Grafo. 'You should have seen the crowds of our people lying in ambush when the devils were flying back! An old woman threw a huge cauldron at one of them and so deftly did she do it the hound was killed on the spot.'

In a voice which did not quite belong to him Idrun asked:

'And what of Ligugé, Master Grafo?'

The innkeeper shrugged.

'From all I have heard, not a stone left on stone there. See, lad, it lies between us and Saintes. What chance would the monks have? There was no armoury either.'

Berno sighed.

'Well, except for seeing you, Grafo, it has been a fruitless journey—my wife needing spices and the lad longing to see Ligugé again.' He shook his head. 'A dearly bought victory indeed!'

'You must not say so abroad,' Grafo broke in. 'The ravaged Poitou will be built up again, and so will Aquitania—they have begun digging wells already. Those unchristened dogs have fouled all we had. No, Master Berno, great good will come out of that battle.'

Suddenly Idrun got up and climbed the steep secret stairs of the Golden Grape. They had saved Grafo's life. Now, as Idrun found himself under the open sky, he breathed freely. Behind him Grifo whispered urgently:

'Come at once. The master wants you.'

Reluctantly Idrun groped down the narrow, slippery stairs. The rushlight fell on Berno's face.

'Son, we are off at dawn. Get what sleep you can.'

'Home, Father?'

'No, we go south,' replied Berno, and said no more.

A heap of rubble and charred stone was all that was left of the great gateway of Ligugé. The basilica and the guest-house had been used for stabling. The spacious sacristies stood there—but all their treasures had vanished. Idrun sought one familiar landmark after another, but so few remained—a kitchen wall standing drunkenly, or a charred cloister arch. Wherever he looked, he saw broken stone on broken stone. The Abbot's lodging was razed to the ground. The whole landscape spoke of wanton and violent destruction, and Idrun wondered how God could have allowed it, but he kept his grief to himself.

At the east end of the great garth they met a few strangers from a hamlet south-west of the Abbey. Idrun kept back, but Berno and the others were led to a great mound to the left of the cross, and Idrun heard one of the strangers say that everything had been done decently.

'We had our priest come here. There they lie. . . . Why, not even the youngest novice was spared by the infidels! Now, masters, all of us have got hatchets and there is no shortage of good timber. Next time you come, there will be a great cross raised over them.'

Idrun, his eyes dry, stared at the mound. There lay his friend, his teacher . . . Idrun felt as though he were being choked by anger and grief. Had Dom Defensor's work been given to the flames? Nothing but cold ashes could be seen in the ruins of the Abbot's lodgings.

'I must find out,' thought Idrun and turned towards the west cloister.

'Young master,' one of the strangers cried shrilly, 'you must not go there. The arches are unsafe—'

But Idrun took no notice, and it pleased him that his father did not call him back.

He had to leap over a mass of broken stone and charred wood before he entered the cloister. Just to the left of him, an arch, its key-stone at a perilous angle, was leaning rather crazily, but that did not deter him.

He stood on the broken flagstones and stared right and left, the acrid breaths of a dead fire all round about him. It seemed impossible to move up or down in that utter desolation, but Idrun clenched his fists and repeated to himself:

'I must find out . . . I must—if it is the very last thing I do.'

At last, after scrambling over heaps of jagged stones, bruising his feet and legs, he found his way into this familiar room. Once there, he looked about, blind despair gripping him. There was nothing to see except charred wood that had once been desk and bookshelves. Piles of ashes littered the floor, so many bad reminders that Ligugé had once possessed a fine library, and Idrun's eyes were misty, but he went down on his knees not to pray but to search. His hands plunged into one pile of burnt parchment after another, and ashes slipped through his fingers. There was nothing at all. The Saracens had done their work with a diabolical thoroughness.

Still on his knees, Idrun laid both hands, palms down, on one such pile. For all he knew, it was all that was left of his master's work. Idrun stayed still. He had no idea how long he had spent in the library. Voices still reached him from the garth, but nobody came near.

He sighed and started his search all over again. A charred wooden binding or two rewarded his efforts. The second search finished, he began on the third, and suddenly he looked at the dark corner farthest from the door. Peering, he saw an enormous pile of rubble which he had not noticed before.

He crept across that ravaged place and plunged both hands into the pile. Stones flew right and left, some were jagged, and Idrun's hands began to bleed, but he went on and on, mouth set. The pile grew smaller and smaller: he had found nothing. Dust all but blinding him, Idrun would not give up.

And then, just before he had got to the very bottom of the pile, he trembled and forgot the pain in his hands. In between two layers of rubble he came on something that was wood, not broken stone. He stooped so low that his face all but touched the rubble. Sweat pouring down his neck and breast, he cleared away what remained and there lay the familiar wooden binding, scratched and dusty but otherwise undamaged.

Idrun's eyes lit up as though the very heavens were opened before him. He scrambled up to his feet, took off his smock, and dried and cleaned both hands most carefully. The left thumb kept bleeding but Idrun hoped that the thick grey linen of the smock would afford enough protection. Then he stooped, turned the clasp and the exquisitely illuminated capital on the first sheet made him shout for joy. Feverishly he began leafing through the volume. Every sheet was intact, and Idrun, oblivious of all else, pressed his great find and kissed the binding.

All the books had been destroyed. This one had escaped, and

Defensor's pupil knew that he had not learned his letters in vain. At Clear Water, within the peace of his little harbour, he would copy the anthology once, twice, three times, and thus pass on his

teacher's gift to the world. left so cruelly ravaged by the Saracens' invasion.

Idrun kept quite still, and for a moment it seemed as though he were no longer alone in that ruined and dishonoured place. The treasure held close to his chest, he began scrambling across the rubble in the cloister. No sooner had he reached the garth when a terrific crash behind made him halt and turn round. The crazily slanted arch had fallen and its fall had brought down three or four more. The way to the west cloister was blocked completely.

He heard frantic shouts from a far distance and, turning, saw Berno, his men and all the strangers running towards him; and Idrun smiled at them all, his bleeding hands holding his treasure.

'What—' began Berno and stopped.

'I have done what I was meant to do, Father,' he said quietly.

They all stared dumbly. One of the strangers scratched his head. 'Young master,' he gasped, 'I did warn you. That arch might have killed you.'

'But I was not meant to be killed,' answered Idrun.